THE DELIVERERS:
SHARKY & THE JEWEL

By

GREGORY S. SLOMBA

Illustrated by Daniel Vogel

I

Published by Gregory S. Slomba in New Fairfield, CT USA

ISBN-13: 978-1461003618
ISBN-10: 146100361X

Printed in the United States of America

To my wife, Stephanie,
for giving me the support and encouragement to take a chance and do
something I always dreamed of doing.

To Deacon Bart,
who first got me to share my writing with
someone other than myself.

Mountain of the Jewel

Table of Contents

CHAPTER I

OUT OF THIS WORLD

The boy's heart hammered in his chest. His knees quaked and he felt weak as he stood on the narrow mountain path, high above the plain below. Wind whipped his red hair and tugged at his clothes, trying to blow him over the cliff as he clung to the solid bulk of the rock face.

Beside him stood a man. Although the face was blurred and indistinct, the boy knew it as his father. The mountaintop was shrouded in mist, making everything around the pair hazy and surreal. A faint reddish light gave the mist a rosy glow, adding to the otherworldly feeling.

The boy's father nodded, and they both began inching up the path, the man in the lead, each clutching the rock face. The boy took a deep breath and looked over the edge of the cliff. Wisps of cloud tracked across his vision, momentarily obscuring, then revealing, the dizzying drop to the landscape below.

He trembled, suddenly unable to move. His father stopped and turned, gesturing for him to follow. Almost without thinking, the boy took one step, then another, then one more. The reddish glow became brighter as they walked, until the air around them glowed blood red.

Suddenly, a black shadow loomed over them. The boy heard the flap of leathery wings and felt a blast of hot air as some creature flew overhead. Startled, both climbers darted toward the cliff to avoid the creature, their momentum carrying them toward the edge. The boy managed to grab hold of a boulder on the precipice, but his father stumbled, wobbled sickeningly on the edge, then toppled over. All the boy could do was watch as his father spun and twisted, hurtling down toward the plain. Arms and legs flailing, the man tumbled, his mouth forming a scream.

"Nooo!!!"

Eric Scott's cry split the night. He sat straight upright, his freckled brow bathed in sweat. Opening his eyes, he stopped screaming and looked around. He was right where he'd been when he'd fallen asleep an hour or so ago—in the blue nylon pup tent under the old oak tree in his back yard.

The light of the full moon and the branches overhead flung shadows across the roof of his little tent. A faint June breeze made the shadows rustle and dance. An owl hooted.

Eric lay back in his sleeping bag, trembling. That dream again. He'd been having the same one ever since his father had died from a fall while hiking, a little over a year ago. It was now so familiar, he knew in his sleep what would happen before it did. The maddening thing was, he could never alter the terrible outcome.

"Probably means I'm next," he muttered. "Man, 12 years old and having nightmares. What am I, a baby?"

He ran a hand through his tousled hair, yawned and stretched. No use trying to get back to sleep, he thought, I'll just send my dad plunging to his death again. Might as well go out and have a look around.

Wriggling out of the sleeping bag, he slipped his long, skinny legs into a pair of jeans and pulled a dark-green sweatshirt on over his blue t-shirt. He crawled over to the tent door and pulled on his socks and sneakers before unzipping the entrance and scrambling out.

The night had turned chilly. Eric stretched again and looked around. The moon provided plenty of light, although a row of trees lining the edge of the yard cast dark shadows in which he could see nothing. The light wind ruffled the grass and played with his hair. The branches of the oak swayed and creaked above him. The sound made him glance up. When he did, he noticed something he'd never seen before.

Perched on the lowest branch, not three feet over his head, was a snowy white owl. It was large. Its eyes were closed, and it appeared to be asleep. Eric stood, transfixed. Wow, an owl, he thought; I've never seen one this close before. Wonder why it's asleep; they're supposed to be nocturnal. It should be hunting.

Its eyes snapped open. Eric held his breath. The owl's large round eyes glinted in the moonlight as it gazed at him for what seemed a long time. Eric tensed, expecting it to fly off, hoping it wouldn't. The owl didn't fly. Instead, it did the last thing Eric expected. It spoke.

"Good evening," it said.

Eric stared at the owl. "You can talk?"

"Obviously," said the owl, "and it appears you can as well."

"People are supposed to talk," Eric said, "but don't expect me to believe owls can."

"My dear boy, I assure you I *am* an owl and, as you can plainly see, I *am* talking."

"Is this some kind of trick?" Eric asked. He looked around, half expecting to see his friends hiding in the bushes.

"Oh, it's no trick," the owl said, with the faintest hint of a smile.

"This is crazy. Animals can't talk, only people."

The owl shook its head. "That's the problem with you humans. You're too full of yourselves. Most of you couldn't care less about talking with us. You don't even take the trouble to find out whether or not we *can* talk, much less if we have anything interesting to say."

"You expect me to believe all owls talk?"

"My dear boy," the owl chuckled. "Not just owls. All animals can speak. Not all of them speak well, mind you, but all speak at least a little. Cats, for instance, are quite well spoken creatures. Dogs tend to blather, saying nothing about everything, while blue jays have a limited vocabulary and are quite nasty. Squirrels are nervous and talk a mile a minute. You humans could hear them if you tried, I daresay, but you simply don't listen."

Eric thought about it a moment. He still didn't completely believe it, but it was hard to deny this particular owl *was* talking.

"Is that your nest?" The owl pointed a wing toward the tent.

"What? Oh, yeah, I guess you could call it that," Eric said. "Do you want to come in and, oh, I don't know, perch a while?"

Perch a while? Did he actually *say* that? Things are getting out of control here, Eric thought.

"Thank you very much, but I prefer the open air. I hope you don't mind."

"Huh? Uh, no, that's okay, it's kinda stuffy in there anyway."

"I much prefer trees, wonderful places to live. I grew up in a tree. Loved it. A nice hollow oak. Very snug."

"Yeah, I guess you'd think so, wouldn't you," Eric said. "This tree of yours, is it near here?"

"No, it is quite far from here. Almost a world away, you might say."

"Well, you know, the tent's not really where I live. I just camp out there." Eric was beginning to think he'd woken up in another dream.

"Then, am I correct in thinking this fine oak is your home?"

Eric laughed. "Are you kidding? I live in that house over there, with my mom." He pointed to his small single-story house.

"There is no need to be impertinent, young man," the owl said, glancing over at the house. "I suppose it was too much to hope you didn't live on the ground. You *are* human after all. Still, you seem to be rather a nice one, despite your prickly disposition. What is your name, if I may ask?"

"It's Eric, Eric Scott. What's yours?"

"My full name is Stigidae Ghostwing, but you may call me Stig."

"Cool name," Eric admitted. "For a bird."

"Yes, it does rather roll off the tongue, if I do say so. I've been watching you—what do you call it? —camp out. Actually, I've been sent to bring you on a little outing being planned, sort of an adventure."

"Oh man, this is too weird," Eric said. "Who sent you, the owl king?"

"My, you certainly woke up on the wrong side of the nest this evening, didn't you?" Stig said, and puffed up his feathers.

"Okay, okay, I'm sorry. Don't get your feathers ruffled," Eric said. "Where's this outing gonna be?"

"Well, it's actually rather close," said Stig. "But then again, it really is quite far away."

"Do all owls talk as crazy as you?" Eric asked, squinting at the owl.

"Well, you see, I'm talking of going to another world."

"You're joking, right?" This is getting weirder and weirder, Eric thought.

"I can understand your skepticism," the owl said. "As a matter of fact, the Gatekeeper said you would make a fuss."

"Where is this world, and who's the Gatekeeper?" Eric asked.

"Well now, those are difficult questions." Stig said, screwing his face into something resembling a frown. "As for the world, it's not here, obviously. To be quite frank, I'm not sure where it is exactly. It's not in this solar system or this universe."

"So it's really far?"

"No, as I said, it's not far from here at all."

"But if it's not even in this universe, how can it be so close?"

"These things *are* rather tricky," Stig said, sighing. "And I don't think it can be easily explained. Let's just say that while worlds can be a universe—or even two—away, there are doorways connecting them that make traveling to them as easy as walking into the next room."

"You mean that there are doorways leading to other worlds in this world?" Eric was getting a headache.

"Not many. Oh, there used to be quite a few, ages ago. There was a time when people would stumble upon them quite regularly and wind up in any number of places, some quite nice and others very terrible. But doorways have been disappearing steadily over the past couple of centuries. I would venture a guess that in this world there remain only a very few."

"You remember?" Eric asked.

"Oh yes, you see, owls live quite a long time where I come from."

"How old are you?"

"Oh let me see...I turned 427, no, no, 428 this past March," Stig said.

"Four hundred twenty-eight," Eric repeated. "Are you sure I'm not dreaming?"

"Quite sure," Stig said. "As I was saying, the number of doorways on each world has been declining. That's where the Gatekeeper comes in. It's he who regulates the traffic to and from worlds."

"You mean people can travel between worlds?" Eric asked, with growing interest.

"Only when the Gatekeeper sends someone on Official Business," the owl said. "Then, they go through a doorway on their world to the Hallway of Worlds. From there, they go to their final destination."

"You mean it's like traveling on the airlines?"

"Er, I really wouldn't know," Stig said.

"What's Official Business?" Eric wanted to know.

"Well, you see, every now and then a world will encounter a problem, a snag, so to speak."

"A snag?" Eric asked.

"Yes, it could be some sort of sociological or technological dilemma, or a stubborn way of thinking—something where some outside help is needed," Stig explained. "Oftentimes all it takes is a little nudge, really, to get things back on track. Some worlds hit a number of snags over the course of their history."

"And this Gatekeeper wants to send me on some Official Business?" Eric asked. A strange excitement coursed through him.

"Actually, he wants to send you and me."

"So you've done this before," Eric said. "Have you ever had any problems?"

"I've had a number of posers, I can tell you," Stig said. "But in the end, I got through them all right."

"Is it dangerous?" Eric asked.

"Well, it's not for the faint of heart, my boy. As a matter of fact," the owl confided, "There was one encounter I had with a giant four-headed ogre that would make your blood run cold. You see, the creature was pillaging the countryside and no one could get at him because, with four heads, he had a perfect panoramic view. Well, I decided to swoop down on him from above and try to peck out his eyes one at a time. How was I to know he would pick that exact moment to look up and check the weather?"

"What did you do?" Eric asked.

"Hmm? Oh, well, it's a little painful to remember, really," Stig said.

"Why?"

"Well, to make a long story short, the beast took a swing at me with its club. Luckily, I managed to avoid it, and the club came smashing down on two of the heads, which restricted its vision a good deal. I took advantage of this by pecking at it with my beak. Fortunately, we were in a mountainous region. I drove the brute over the nearest cliff and that was that."

"Man, that was a little harsh, don't you think?" Eric said.

"No more harsh than what that creature was dealing out to the gentle folk of the area," Stig replied.

"So the Gatekeeper needs me?" Eric's brow furrowed, but his heart leaped.

"Oh my, yes," Stig said. "He was most specific."

"If I go, how will I get back?"

"The Gatekeeper will send you back through the proper door," Stig said. "It's really quite simple."

Eric nodded. It's hard to believe I'm even considering this, he thought. "I guess I could go and check it out, at least."

Stig clapped his wings in delight. "Splendid, splendid. I'm so glad. Now come along, we must be going."

"Where?" asked Eric.

"Through the doorway. Follow me," Stig said, and soared into the air.

"Hey wait! I can't fly!" Eric called.

"Well hurry." Stig said as he circled the boy. "We've wasted enough time already."

"I gotta get some stuff!" Eric ran into the tent, shoved his flashlight, some rope and a canteen into his knapsack, slung it over his shoulder, and hurried out after the owl. He was just in time to see Stig's white body disappearing over the house toward the front yard.

Eric caught up with him at a row of trees that lined the steep slope of his front lawn where it fell down to a stream. The owl descended, and Eric plunged into the thick undergrowth that grew on the hillside. Pricker bushes pulled at his pants legs as he scrambled down. A bed of old leaves made the ground slippery, and hidden rocks and roots threatened to trip him in the dark.

When he reached the bottom, he heard the stream gurgling and chattering as it flowed in its bed. It was wide and shallow, and Eric could not help remembering the times he and his father had caught frogs and crawfish in the muddy water. Stig was waiting for him on a big rock in the middle.

"Got down okay?" asked Stig.

"Oh sure," said Eric, plucking a thorn from his leg. "No trouble, just a bit steep is all."

"Right, well the easy part is over. From now on, remember that anything can happen! And I daresay, it probably will!" Stig appeared to be smiling, but in the tricky light of the moon it was hard to be sure. "This next bit will be a little wet for you, I'm afraid, but it won't last very long. Just keep slogging ahead, and you'll get there in no time."

"Wet? What do you mean, wet?" asked Eric, but Stig was off, flying along the brook.

Eric shrugged his shoulders and followed. They headed up along the stream and he could see the stone retaining wall and the large drainpipe that passed under his driveway.

Stig, flying a little ahead, called over his shoulder, "Into the drainpipe!" and swooped straight into the dark opening.

The pipe was four feet in diameter. Eric stepped onto a flat rock standing in the water and peered into the opening.

"Come on!" Stig's voice echoed from inside. "We're almost there."

"It's kind of dark, isn't it?" This was definitely weird. Who ever heard of walking into a drainpipe in the middle of the night?

"It won't hurt you," said Stig. "My wings are getting tired. Are you coming?"

"Yeah, keep your feathers on," said the boy as he stepped onto the lip of the pipe.

He had to bend over because the pipe was too short for him to stand upright. He had expected to see a faint light coming from the other side, but it was black up ahead. He made his way forward as his eyes adjusted. His sneakers and socks were wet and squishy as he made his way along the ribbed interior of the pipe. Then he saw the white owl up ahead, a ghostly shape of lighter darkness.

"Now what?" asked Eric.

"We're here," said Stig. "We're at the doorway."

"Already? Where?"

Stig pointed with his wing, and there it was—the faint outline of a round door filling the end of the drainpipe. Eric blinked with surprise. It was here, in his front yard.

In all his exploring, he had never seen it. He was positive the door hadn't been there before.

"I've never seen this," Eric said in wonder.

"Of course you haven't," said Stig. "A Doorway appears only if the Gatekeeper wants it to be seen. Now would you mind opening the door for me? It's terribly difficult to do with wings."

Eric pushed on the door, they went forward, and a moment later it swung shut behind them. In awe, Eric gaped around him. They were in a long corridor with doors on either side, each one the same. He noticed that the door they had just come through had shifted to match the others, all rectangles about seven feet high with a large pane of frosted glass in the top half.

The hallway was lit by many chandeliers hanging from the ceiling, each of which held many candles that burned without a flicker in the still air. A red velvet carpet covered the floor, and it stretched as far as he could see, seeming to go on forever in both directions.

Then, with a flicker of light, a desk materialized on his right. A wizened man with a long white beard and golden spectacles was sitting behind it. The desk was littered with papers. A large white quill pen stood in a jar of India ink amid the clutter. The man smiled as he rubbed his hands together. His blue eyes sparkled as he looked at the boy and the owl.

"Well, well, so this is the young man, is it, Stig?" he asked.

"Yes, quite correct," said Stig as he landed on the desk. "I have the honor of presenting Master Eric Scott. Eric, this is the Gatekeeper."

The old man stood up, his blue robes shimmering, and offered Eric a bony hand.

"Very pleased to meet you, my boy," he said.

"Uh, same here," said Eric, shaking the old man's hand. He had expected the Gatekeeper to have a weak grip like his grandfather's, and was surprised by its strength.

The old man grinned as if reading his thoughts. "This job keeps me on the move," he said. "It wouldn't do to get out of shape. Now, I suppose Stig has explained all this to you. Is that right?" The Gatekeeper's voice assumed a serious tone.

"Yeah, I think so," Eric frowned. "Um, he told me about going through the Doorway into the Hallway and meeting you and being sent on Official Business and all. I'm still not sure that this is for me, though." The Gatekeeper's sudden change of mood had made him very unsure of himself. Until he had entered the Hallway, Eric still had thought he could back out if he wanted. Now, he wasn't so sure.

The Gatekeeper's eyes regarded him intently. "Well, since you know the basics, let me tell you a little about the task at hand. If you have any doubts, say the word and I'll send you back home and that's the end of it. From the look of you, I'd say you'll be able to make up your own mind. Does that sound all right?"

Eric nodded, his fears allayed somewhat.

"Okay, lovely." The Gatekeeper broke into another wide grin. "The task involves a small fishing village called Calendria. The village is prey to a band of pirates that keeps them as virtual slaves to supply them with food and other goods."

"Why don't they fight back?" Eric asked.

"The majority don't because they live in constant fear of the pirates' captain, Sharky, who has led his crew for almost three hundred years."

"Three hundred years?" Eric wasn't sure he'd heard right.

The Gatekeeper nodded. "He wields a terrible power, one that gives him long life. Many villagers also believe he can see straight into their minds and hearts, and that resistance would be futile. Some, however, believe otherwise and are working to resist him."

"But what can I do?" Eric asked.

"Maybe nothing," the Gatekeeper replied. "But Calendria is the lynchpin of this particular world. If it remains under Sharky's dominion, the entire world will be subject to a darker power and won't survive."

"You mean you want me to save the village, maybe the world?" Eric asked. "I'm not Superman."

"Well, of course you aren't," said the Gatekeeper. "That's why I'm sending Stig with you. The two of you should be able to handle things."

Eric looked at Stig. The owl's large golden eyes gazed back. The boy frowned. Well, now what, he thought. The chance to explore another world, visit a place no one on earth had been was something that made him quiver with excitement. Then why did he hesitate? Because, he thought, I'm scared to death. Me? Fight pirates? Take on supernatural powers? Eric looked from the impassive face of the Gatekeeper to Stig, who winked at him.

Eric faced the Gatekeeper. "But why *me?*"

"Because," the Gatekeeper replied, "I need someone who's brave and has the confidence to stick with what he believes. You're just the one to convince others that you're right. Above all, though, I need someone who won't give in to fear."

"But that's not me. I...I couldn't even save my dad," Eric's eyes flashed a defiance that suddenly faded. He hung his head. "I was too busy worrying about myself."

"Listen to me, boy," the Gatekeeper's voice was so sharp that Eric flinched. "What happened to your father wasn't your fault. There wasn't anything you could have done to keep him from falling, so don't beat yourself up about it."

"You know about my dad?" Eric blinked.

"Of course; it's all here in your file." The Gatekeeper patted a thin folder that lay on the desk. "You and your father were hiking last year. You scrambled up onto a ledge; your father followed. Part of the ledge gave way, and he fell. You see, I've had my eye on you for a while now. You say you don't have what I'm looking for, but you're wrong." The old man's face softened, and he smiled gently. "The day will come when you'll find there's more about you than you can guess. Now, what do you say?"

Eric took a deep breath, fighting back tears. The old man thought he knew the whole story, but he was wrong. Eric knew. He'd grabbed a boulder instead of his father's outstretched hand. If he hadn't been so afraid, his father would still be alive. But there was something about the Gatekeeper, and Stig too, that he couldn't turn his back on.

"Okay, I'll do it," he whispered. His voice gave no hint of the eagerness and fear that churned within him. He silently hoped the old man knew what he was talking about.

The Gatekeeper smiled. "Splendid! I knew I made the right choice."

"Hoo, hoo!" hooted Stig, momentarily losing his calm and quite a few feathers as he flapped his wings. "I'm so glad. It will be so much better than having to do it alone."

"So, what happens now?" Eric asked.

"Follow me." The old man started off up the corridor. "Let's see, so many doors..."

He looked to the left and right as he led them along, trying to see through the frosted glass and muttering to himself. Eric's wet sneakers felt cold and clammy, and made squishing sounds with each step he took. Every now and then the Gatekeeper would stop for a minute, then shake his head and move on.

"It's here somewhere," he said over his shoulder. Then he stopped short and peered at a door on the left. "Ah, here it is!" he said.

"How can he tell?" Eric whispered to Stig, who was hovering beside him. "That door looks just like all the others."

"I don't know, but he's never wrong," Stig whispered back. "As a matter of fact, I do believe he does all that hemming and hawing just for show. He can be a little overly dramatic at times."

The Gatekeeper turned and smiled. "This is the place. Any final questions before you go through? No? Then good luck to the both of you, and I'll see you when your task is done.

"Farewell Eric. Go with your instincts and believe in yourself! Bye, bye, Stig. You've done splendidly in the past. That should come in handy here."

He opened the door and ushered them through.

CHAPTER 2

CALENDRIA

Eric and Stig stepped into a lush tropical jungle. Eric heard the chatter of monkeys hidden in the trees, the distant calls of birds, and the babble of running water.

Then he heard the door shut. He whipped around and saw only jungle. The door was gone.

"That's the way it always is," said Stig. "The door disappears until we finish the Assignment."

Eric felt a stab of fear. Jungles. Pirates. What was he doing here? "Umm, now what?" His voice came out a bit creaky.

Stig settled on a jagged tree stump. "We need to find that village. I'll fly up and have a look around."

"No!" He cried. Stig couldn't leave him alone in this strange place. Then, embarrassed, he mumbled, "Uh, I mean, I think it'd be safer if we kept together. Let's find the stream I hear."

Stig peered at him for a long moment, then said gently, "Very well."

The rushing sound of water seemed to come from the left, so they struck out in that direction, pushing their way through vine-draped trees and dense undergrowth. It was hot, tough going, even for Stig, whose wings were useless in the thick growth. He hopped from branch to branch while Eric stumbled over hidden roots, and brushed leaves and cobwebs from his face and hair.

At last they broke through onto the bank of a clear shallow river, tumbling over small, smooth rocks. Eric flopped down on his knees and took a long drink. Stig landed on the mossy bank and pecked at the water with his beak. His thirst satisfied, Eric wiped his dripping face and looked around.

"Stig," he said, "There aren't as many trees along the stream and almost no vines; it'd be easier to travel along the stream."

"I say, that's an excellent idea," said Stig. He looked up and down the stream. "But, er, which way should we go?"

Eric thought, then he remembered something his father had told him on one of their camping trips. "We should follow the current. A lot of streams and rivers flow into larger bodies of water. If we want to find a fishing village, it's probably beside a lake or an ocean. The stream might lead us there."

"Wonderful," Stig said. "Lead the way."

They made their way downstream, following the current. Fewer trees and less underbrush made for easier going. With less cover, the sun was hot but, thanks to the stream, they had all the water they needed to keep them cool. After traveling for a short time, the trees came to a sudden end, and they emerged from the jungle onto a long stretch of beach that led down to an ocean. Waves washed over the sand.

The beach stretched a great distance to their left, before it curved back around behind them and out of sight. To the right, it went a long way until it bent out toward the sea to form either an outcrop of land or another stretch of beach—Eric couldn't tell from where he stood. The jungle ended where the beach began to curve. From there on, the ground rose and was very rocky. Eric looked back at the jungle. Beyond it, stretching in either direction as far as he could see, loomed a range of very tall mountains, their snowcapped peaks wreathed in cloud.

Eric scanned the beach in both directions, his hand shading his eyes. Besides the wind blowing the trees and the surf pounding the beach, nothing moved. Stig landed on a large piece of driftwood. Eric sat down beside him.

"What now?" Eric asked.

"I could fly on down the beach and see what's beyond that ridge," Stig suggested.

"I guess so," said Eric, who still had misgivings about being on his own. "That village probably isn't that far away."

"Right," said Stig. "I'll be back presently."

Just then, they heard a rustle in the jungle, and a dozen brightly colored birds flew into the air in every direction. Eric jumped to his feet and Stig took to the air as a small figure clad in what looked like a rumpled blue sack came running out of the jungle. It rushed up and its bare feet slid in the sand as it came to a stop a few feet away from them. Two small hands held a bow and arrow trained on Eric. Two piercing violet eyes glinted at him from under a mop of tousled black hair. Then it spoke in a high-pitched voice that, though fierce, Eric knew could belong only to a girl.

"Don't move a muscle, spy, or my arrow will pierce your heart!"

Eric could now see that the blue sack was actually a skirt that was rumpled and dirty from the girl's trek through the jungle. A palm frond peeked out of a torn sleeve of the white blouse she wore. Her outfit reminded Eric of one he had seen at a colonial village he had visited with his mother. The girl was just a little shorter than he and looked to be about his age.

"Spy?" he asked, bewildered.

"Yeah, pirate spy," she said, and gestured with her bow and arrow toward Stig, who hovered in the air beside Eric. "I saw you and your parrot sneaking around the beach."

"You're nuts," Eric scoffed. "We weren't sneaking, and this isn't a parrot. His name is Stig. He's my friend, not my pet."

Stig returned to his perch, his feathers ruffled. "I should say not! Parrot, how perfectly ridiculous. Imagine mistaking an owl for a parrot. I've never been so insulted! Put your archery set away this instant, young lady. You're liable to injure someone."

Now it was the girl's turn to look confused. She lowered her homemade bow slightly while blowing her hair out of her face. She gave Stig a hard stare.

"What kind of bird are you?" she asked. "Parrots repeat what their masters say, but I've never heard of one that can talk on its own."

"I should say you haven't, young lady," said Stig. "I daresay there are none in the vicinity that can."

"Stig's kinda special," Eric said.

"He's bewitched." She paused, and Eric thought her whole body quivered. "Who are you?"

"Not pirates, that's for sure," Eric said.

"Are you the heroes of the legend?" Her hands shook so much, she nearly dropped the bow.

"Heroes?" Eric asked. "We're not heroes, we were sent..."

"You are! I knew it! What else could you be—a boy with strange clothes and a talking bird. You'd have to be. It's not quite like the legend. I mean, you're no warrior and your bird isn't as fierce as an eagle, but still, who else could you be? I've been searching for you every day; in the jungle, on the beaches, ever since I had the dream. I'd almost given up hope. Papa told me to be patient, help would come when the time was right. But I couldn't keep still; I was too excited!"

26

All of a sudden, she stopped. "Papa! He's going to want to meet you."

She grabbed Eric by the hand and started to pull him toward the jungle. Eric dug in his heels and yanked his hand from her grasp.

"Wait a second," he said. "What's this all about? What legend? Who's your papa?"

"And, more to the point," chimed in Stig, "where are we?"

"You mean, you don't know?" asked the girl.

Eric and Stig exchanged glances. "No," they said in unison.

"We were told about a village called Calendria and about pirates who kept the villagers as slaves, but besides that, we don't know anything," Eric said.

"That's right," the girl's head bobbed up and down. "The pirates have been terrifying Calendria for ages. The whole village lives in terror of their raids."

"Yeah, so like I said, that's about all we know," said Eric, shrugging his shoulders.

"Then we've got to see my papa right away," said the girl. "He'll tell you everything and then you can tell him how you're going to help."

"Uh, yeah, sure," said Eric. He gave Stig a questioning look.

"I do think that's best," Stig said. "But first, I should like to know your name, my girl."

"I'm called Kate, Kate Endria," said the girl.

"I'm Eric and this is Stigidae Ghostwing, Stig for short."

"How do you do?" Stig asked.

"Well, thank you," Kate answered.

"You're well mannered, whatever else," said Stig. "Although perhaps a trifle excitable. There, now that the introductions are out of the way, I suppose we'd best be moving along."

"Okay, Calendria is by a bay, around that headland," she pointed to the spit of land Eric had noticed earlier. "But from here it's quicker to go through the jungle, and there's less chance of being seen."

"By who?" Eric asked.

"Sharky," Kate whispered with such intensity that, without thinking, Eric glanced around. "It's a known fact that Sharky's always watching. It's not wise to spend too long in the open. C'mon."

She led them up the beach toward the trees. They plunged in, out of the sunshine and back into the dimmer light of the dense foliage. The stifling closeness of the trees seemed to be impenetrable, but Kate wove her way around all obstacles, avoiding every grove of tangled vines and clump of twisted trees they encountered. Eric thought they were angling to the left of the point where they had entered the jungle, but with all the detours they took he couldn't be sure. Soon the ground began to rise and grow steeper, until they came out into a bright, sunlit clearing.

Eric became dizzy as he saw they had crested the hill and now stood on top of a ridge. On the right, the ridge stretched for about a hundred yards before sloping down to the foot of the mountain range they had seen from the beach. The mountains ran like a wall, straight and tall, as far as Eric could see. When he looked to the left, he saw that the ridge stretched in and around, forming the headland they'd seen earlier. The bay was shaped like a horseshoe with an identical headland on the far side.

"That's Calendria," Kate pointed toward the bay.

Looking down, they saw a small village of shops, cottages and farms nestled by the water. There was a wharf on the water, where several fishing boats were moored. The land around the town was dotted with a number of small farms. A river flowed from the mountains to the sea down below them, powering a grist mill. An arched stone bridge spanned the waterway, most likely, Eric thought, to bring carts and livestock into the village from the outlying farms.

As he looked down the steep slope into the valley below, his knees buckled and he began to tremble.

"What's the matter?" Kate had noticed his shaking.

"Uh, nothing. What makes you think anything's wrong?" Eric said, trying to be cool. He wasn't about to let a girl know he was scared of heights.

Kate gave him a strange look. "We'd better get off this ridge; we're too exposed." She led them down a worn footpath, which gradually became a proper road that ran by the valley farms. Eric hurried after her.

The farmhouses and outbuildings were made of stone and the roofs were thatched. Stone walls divided the fields where spring planting was taking place from those where cattle and sheep grazed. Kate seemed to know everyone they saw, calling out greetings to each as she passed.

The farmers waved and returned her greeting from wherever they were working in the fields; whether from behind a plow pulled by a team of oxen, or from their knees amid the vegetables.

After passing through the farmland, they came to the river and the stone bridge. The bridge was a large structure of cut stone that arched high over the middle of the water, and descended to the other side. The stone was worn smooth by the comings and goings of generation after generation of farmers and their livestock. Kate led them onto the bridge and Eric followed, finding the smooth stones slightly lumpy through his sneakers.

When he had reached the top of the arch, Eric stopped and turned to look upstream. The river flowed from the mountains, cascading down in a huge waterfall before gurgling and bubbling down the valley, under the bridge, past the grist mill and out to the sea.

"That's Tumbledown Falls," said Kate, "and those are the Iron Mountains. Our village has an iron mine at the base of that mountain over there." She pointed to a particularly tall peak, its summit hidden in the clouds.

"What's beyond the mountains?" asked Eric. To him, they looked intimidating, snowcapped and wreathed in cloud as they were. They seemed to be even more of an impenetrable wall from ground level.

"Don't know," Kate replied. "No one from our village has ever found a way over them. Everyone says they're too high."

"It doesn't sound as if you feel that way," said Stig.

"One day, I'm going to do it," said Kate, her violet eyes glittered with a faraway look. "I'm going to climb over or go through, or whatever, and discover all sorts of places. There's bound to be something interesting behind them."

"And you're not worried about the danger?" asked Stig. "Or the fact that no one's made it through?"

"Papa laughs whenever I start talking about going beyond the mountains, like it's some kind of joke," Kate became very red in the face. "Everybody laughs and says it can't be done, but I'll do it, just you wait."

Eric didn't think he'd be able to climb a mountain, but he kept the thought to himself. Instead, he said, "I can't see one girl climbing to the top of that mountain."

"Well, at least I don't get dizzy on the top of a little ridge," Kate retorted.

"Might I remind you two that there are more important things at the moment than mountain-climbing expeditions?" Stig asked. "Perhaps you've forgotten about Sharky and the pirates? I daresay

30

they're going to be a big enough problem on their own. We'd best get on."

Kate led Eric and Stig down the other side of the bridge and into the village itself. The dirt road took them past a few in-town farms that were smaller than their neighbors across the river. They soon came to what looked to Eric to be the main road. It was paved with cobblestones and intersected the road they were traveling, forming a cross. Looking to his left, Eric could see that the road led down to the sea. To the right, it sloped uphill.

"This way," said Kate, and turned right. "I live on the Green."

They followed her through the village. The wood and stone houses were set close together. They looked bright and cheery, and many of the front windows were open to catch the summer air. Each had a small patch of ground in front that most residents used as a garden.

At the top of the hill, the street split in two to form a square. In the center was the town green. It was a little smaller than a football field, and dotted with trees. Livestock grazed there. A large statue of a man in what looked like hiking gear stood in the center of the Green. Various businesses lined the street around the Green. Eric saw signs indicating an apothecary, shoemaker, tailor, printer, potter, cooper, blacksmith, tinsmith, bank, butcher, and baker, among others.

"Where do you live?" Eric asked Kate.

"Over there," she said, and pointed to a large house on the far side of the green. It was much larger than any of the other houses he had seen. It reminded him of a small colonial mansion, and was painted white with black shutters. A walkway of red brick led to the front door, and was bordered on either side by lush gardens.

"Geez," said Eric. "What does your papa do?"

"He's the Lord Mayor," said Kate.

CHAPTER 3

THE LORD MAYOR

Kate led the way, walking so fast that Eric had a hard time keeping up. When she was halfway there, Kate ran the rest of the way across the Green and up the brick walk to the front door, and turned to wait for them to catch up, shifting from one foot to another. Stig flew after Kate, circling her head once before landing on a small bench by the door. Eric tore after them both and arrived slightly out of breath and embarrassed about being last, although he tried not to let it show.

"When we go in," said Kate, "I'll explain things to Papa, and then you can give him your plan for handling the pirates."

What plan? Eric thought.

Kate opened the door and led them into the house. When Eric stepped inside, he nearly gasped in awe. He'd never been anywhere so fancy, except maybe a museum. A curved staircase of shiny dark wood dominated the entrance hall. The morning sun sparkled on a large chandelier that hung from the ceiling. Two portraits in large golden frames hung above a dark carved sideboard on which sat finely painted vases, crystal candlesticks and other delicate items. Eric edged away from it, not wanting to risk bumping into it and breaking something. A wide arch on the left led to another room that Eric guessed to be the living room. The house was silent except for the ticking of a large grandfather clock by the stairs.

Kate picked up a small silver bell from the sideboard and rang it once. In a few moments, a frowning woman came down the stairs. She wore a long black dress that hid her feet, and a white apron. Her gray-streaked brown hair was tied back in a bun. She looked down her pointed nose at them, her mouth a thin line. Her eyebrows went up when she caught sight of Stig, who had perched on the sideboard.

"Mistress Kate, what have you been up to?" She asked in a disapproving tone, and pointed to Stig, "The house is no place for wildlife, and you should ask your father's permission before bringing strange children into the house." She looked at Eric, "Where do you come from, boy? I don't believe I know you."

Kate rolled her eyes. "Oh, Gretchen. How do you know I haven't asked Papa? Anyway, he said if I ever found anything that might help, I should bring it home. That's what I've done, and we've got to see him right away!"

"Your father is not to be disturbed, young lady," Gretchen said. "He has a great deal of work to do."

"But this is important!" Kate huffed. "He wanted me to let him know if I ever found something, and I have."

"Kate, it will have to wait. I don't care what you've found. Your father is in his study working. Now, I want you and your friend to take that bird and go play on the Green. I'll call you when it's time for supper; you can talk to him then."

"My dear lady," Stig took a couple steps closer to Gretchen along the sideboard and fluffed his feathers. "It really is a matter of utmost urgency that we talk to his Lordship."

The maid went very pale and began to shake. "Mmmmistress Kate, is this some kind of a trick?"

33

"No, Gretchen, this is Stig, and the young man is Eric. They've come to help us. That's why I really need to speak with Papa right away."

"Wh—, wha—, um, yes, er, I see that. I'll get him s-straightaway. M-miss Kate, take your guests into the drawing room." She scurried away.

Kate led them through the arch Eric had noticed earlier into a large but comfortable room with two big, cushy sofas, a couple of wing chairs and a few tables. On the wall across from the arch Eric saw a striking portrait of a beautiful woman with violet eyes and a dazzling smile that hung over the fireplace. Eric thought the woman's black hair almost glowed.

"That's Mama," Kate said when she noticed Eric staring. "Her name was Olivia. She died when I was seven."

"Oh, I'm terribly sorry," Stig landed on the mantle over the fireplace for a closer look. "A beautiful woman."

"Yeah," Eric murmured and added, "My dad died last year."

"I miss Mama," Kate said, gazing at the picture. "Sometimes I come in here at night when I can't sleep and talk to her."

"Talk to her?" Eric snorted. "That's silly. I don't talk to pictures of my dad. Whoever heard of talking to a picture?"

Kate shot him a fiery look. "Well maybe you should try it; it might make you less bitter."

"I'm not bitter, just sensible." Why did girls have to be such… girls he thought.

"Children, please! Don't argue," Stig cut in. "We don't want to get off on the wrong claw, do we?"

"He started it," Kate snapped.

"Did not! Girls!" Eric fumed.

"We can discuss this some other time," Stig said. "For the present, we must keep our minds on the task at hand. Do you have any other family, child?"

"No, it's just Papa and me," Kate sighed. "Gretchen takes care of us. She's strict, but she can be sweet at times. Papa's wonderful. Since my dream, he's let me spend all my spare time on patrol, except on Tariff Day."

"What's that?" Eric asked.

"The day the pirates come," Kate scowled. "It happens twice a year, once in the spring and once at harvest. They take half of everything we produce."

"Everything?" Eric asked, startled.

"Half of what we grow, the livestock, clothes, shoes, medicine, tools and everything else we make."

"But why?" Eric asked.

"To keep them from plundering Calendria," said a deep voice behind them.

Startled, all three turned. Standing in the doorway was a tall man with jet-black hair graying at the temples and a close-clipped beard. His brown eyes were bright but sad, Eric thought. He wore a blue coat over a white shirt and a red sash around his waist. The end of the sash hung down along the right leg of his black breeches. His white stockings reached up to just below his knees, like men Eric had seen in paintings from colonial times

"Papa!" Kate yelled and ran into his open arms.

"So, my little ragamuffin, what have you been up to?" the Lord Mayor asked. He smiled as he hugged his daughter.

"I've brought the heroes, Papa," She pointed at Eric and Stig. "I found them, just like I did in my dream."

35

"Heroes, you say?" He looked Eric and Stig over, his eyes intent. "I see only a boy and a bird."

"An owl," Kate said.

"Hardly heroes, my dear."

"But he has such strange clothes, and..." she paused for effect. "The owl can talk."

The Lord Mayor walked over to the fireplace and peered at Stig. The owl stared back, his golden eyes unblinking.

"He *is* a peculiar creature. I can't recall ever seeing a bird of this type before."

"I have always found humans as a whole to be an exceedingly peculiar species as well, thank you," Stig said.

The Lord Mayor gasped. "So, Kate is correct. You *can* talk."

"Quite so," Stig replied. "She seems to have equated the boy and me with one of your legends—something about a warrior and an eagle."

The Lord Mayor nodded. "The Deliverers. It's one of her favorites, and ever since having a dream about finding them two weeks ago, she has spent all her time searching."

"And I've found them, Papa!" Kate blurted. "Who else could they be?"

"Well, it seems you've found something, my dear." The Lord Mayor's eyes narrowed as he studied Eric and Stig. "I'll give you that. The question is, what?

The Lord Mayor suddenly smiled and extended his hand. "But where are my manners? Charles Endria, Lord Mayor of Calendria, at your service."

Eric held out his hand, and the Lord Mayor shook it with a firm grip. "Uh, Eric Scott, nice to meet you."

"And my name is Stigidae Ghostwing, Stig for short." He extended a wing, which the Lord Mayor shook.

"Sit, please, here on the couch," the Lord Mayor said. "Kate, ask Gretchen to bring in some refreshments."

Kate ran out of the room. Eric sat down on a couch, while the Lord Mayor settled into a wing chair. Stig perched on a table between them.

Kate came back into the room carrying a plate of cookies. Gretchen followed with a tray of glasses filled with what looked to Eric like lemonade. As Gretchen set her tray down on the table, she gave Stig a sideways glance.

"Will there be anything else, sir?"

"Not now. Thanks, Gretchen," the Lord Mayor smiled.

"Very good, sir. I'll just get back to my sweeping then." She gave Stig and Eric another queer look and left the room.

"Please help yourself," the Lord Mayor said.

Eric poured a few sips of his lemonade onto a plate for Stig. He hadn't realized how hungry he was, and was tempted to take a handful of cookies, but took only a couple. "Uh, Kate started telling us about the pirates and Tariff Day, and she said something about a legend, umm, the Deliverers."

"So, my daughter has given you an indication of what troubles Calendria?"

"I didn't have a chance to tell them all that much, really," Kate said.

"Well, if Kate is right and you have been sent to help us, then you need to know the entire story," the Lord Mayor said. "It's long. In fact, it spans the entire history of this village.

"Calendria was settled almost three hundred years ago by a band of pirates who had grown tired of the life and wanted to find a bit of land and retire. Their leader was a man by the name of Calvin Endria, my ancestor. These pirates and their families—"

"Pirates have families?" Eric asked.

"Oh yes. They're human, after all. Anyway, these pirates were part of a larger band of 200 or so. Endria was the first mate. Their home port was a rock island riddled with caves in which they lived and hid their stolen loot.

"Endria wanted to retire. He'd scouted around a bit during raids and spotted an ideal location for a village. As you can see, we have a sheltered bay opening into the sea for sailing and fishing, open fields for farming, drinking water that runs down from the mountains and—most important of all—a range of tall mountains that cut us off from the rest of the mainland, preventing an attack from behind by any other hostile folk. Endria presented his idea to about forty like-minded members of the crew who enthusiastically promised their support. It then fell to him to make their intentions known to the captain.

"Now, the captain's name was Burt Sharky, a cunning devil with a heart as black as they come. In fact, it was rumored among the crew that he had no real heart at all, just a lump of coal. He'd just as soon kill you as look at you, unless there was something in it for him."

"Geez," Eric exclaimed, "No wonder Endria and his band wanted out of Sharky's crew. But Sharky doesn't sound like the kind of guy who would appreciate desertion."

The Lord Mayor nodded. "Endria realized that. He knew he had to make it worth the captain's while. So, he proposed that if his group were allowed to settle somewhere off on its own, they would pay a tariff twice a year."

"You mean what you pay on Tariff Day," Eric said.

"That's right," the Lord Mayor said, nodding. "Half of all they produced for a hundred years. Sharky was torn between agreeing to the deal and having Endria and his group killed, but he decided to take the offer."

"But you said the village has been paying the Tariff for close to three hundred years," Eric said. "Why are you still paying it?"

Kate rolled her eyes. "Because, Sharky broke the agreement."

"He never intended to end the Tariff when the agreement was up," the Lord Mayor explained. "He turned up on what should have been the last Tariff Day with a new weapon, black powder."

"So how can Sharky live so long?" Eric asked. "Is he immortal?"

"Not immortal, but something very close to it," the Lord Mayor said. "He possesses a gold ring in which is set a gem that gleams with an evil red fire. Some say it allows him to see into the minds of men. Perhaps it's the cause of his unnaturally long life. At any rate, that is what has kept us under his thumb all these years. Even if we were to withstand his black powder, there is no way for us to defeat Sharky himself."

Eric put down the cookie he was eating, his appetite gone. Stig, however, remained unfazed. "We'll just have to see about that, won't we."

"So, you think Sharky can be killed?" the Lord Mayor asked.

"Every living creature I have ever encountered is mortal, and, I daresay, Eric can say the same, isn't that right, my boy?"

"What? Oh, yeah, sure," Eric answered. "What's this black powder?"

"An explosive substance that's packed into a cylindrical machine called a cannon, along with an iron ball. When the powder is ignited, it shoots the ball great distances."

His thoughts were racing—a 300-year-old pirate and gunpowder and cannon threatening a village that he had to save. He needed time to think.

"Sir, uh, Kate mentioned something about a legend."

"That started not long after Sharky broke his word," the Lord Mayor said. "An old woman who lived on one of the outlying farms claimed to have dreamed of a mighty hero from another world who delivered the village from the pirates. He was seven feet tall and was accompanied by an eagle that had the gift of speech. The hero had a mighty weapon that he used to defeat the pirates and the black powder, while the eagle grabbed Sharky in its great talons and dropped him into the sea. The legend spread through the village like wildfire and has been told and retold over the past two centuries. We call the two heroes the Deliverers."

"Man," said Eric, "That's a wild story, but what does that have to do with us?"

Kate shook her head and looked at Eric as if he had no clue. "You two are the heroes in the legend. You're obviously not from this world—I've never seen clothes like yours before and your bird talks, not like a pirate's parrot, he actually thinks."

"I told you before, he's not *my* bird," Eric said, getting annoyed. "He's my friend. And I'm not a hero; I'm just a kid, and I don't know what I can do to help you fight a whole army of pirates. Maybe Stig has some ideas, but I sure don't, so don't get your hopes up." He slumped back in the sofa and nibbled at a cookie.

Stig turned to the Lord Mayor. "I think my young friend is worried that your daughter is putting too much faith in us. Frankly, at this point, I'm not sure what we are supposed to do, but I do know that we are here for a reason, and we do intend to help as much as we can."

The Lord Mayor looked at them both from under dark, bushy eyebrows. He stood like that for so long, Eric was tempted to pinch him to snap him out of it. Then the Lord Mayor nodded his head. "Right," he said. "I accept your offer. Like you, I don't know what you can do. I don't know if you really are the Deliverers, but I can't say for certain that you're not."

Stig and Eric stared at each other.

"So what happens now?" Eric asked.

"I'm going to call an emergency session of the village Council for tonight," the Lord Mayor said. "We'll see what they think."

"When is the next Tariff Day?" Eric asked.

"In about two months. The spring tariff was a couple of months ago, so that gives us some time. If nothing else, I believe your coming is a sign that we must take action. Maybe that's all you need to do."

Eric frowned. "Could be."

"Kate, dinner won't be for a few hours yet. Why don't you take our guests and show them around the village," the Lord Mayor said.

Kate's face broke into a delighted grin.

"But keep who they are, or who you think they are, to yourself," her father cautioned.

Kate's face fell again. "All right, Papa," she said.

She led them out of the house and across the Green. They walked down the main street and across the intersection that led to the river and the farms, passing a large wooden pen half full of cattle, pigs, goats and sheep. Each species was fenced in its own section. The air carried the pungent smell of livestock.

"Whose animals are those?" Eric asked, wrinkling his nose.

"The stockyards," Kate said. "The farmers bring the animals that they want to sell to market once a month. The pens are usually fuller, but there are always fewer animals after Tariff Day."

"How does Tariff Day work?" Eric asked.

"Everyone is expected to bring half of what they make down to the wharf. So, the blacksmith brings half the tools he's made during the winter, the butcher half of what he's slaughtered, the farmers half of the livestock born or crops grown, depending on the time of year. Sharky and his men wait at the wharf and collect everything. Every family's name is printed in a ledger, and Captain Sharky writes what they've brought beside their name."

"What keeps them from bringing less than half?" Eric asked.

"With his ring, Sharky can always tell. Some have tried to give less than half, but they're always caught." Kate made a face. "You don't want to short the Tariff."

"What do they do, kill you?" Eric asked.

"No, that would cut down on the amount of the provisions," Kate's eyes narrowed. "They flog you—you know, with a whip—so many lashes for the men, a little less for the women, and a few for the children."

"They whip the children, too?" Eric's eyes widened.

"Yeah, so there's not too many people who want to try and short the Tariff."

The cobblestone street became a sandy lane, then ended as they approached the wharf. The ground near the harbor was made of crushed seashells, sand and dirt held back by a stone retaining wall. Five or six weather-beaten buildings lined the small port. Eric saw signs for a shipwright, a net weaver, a sail maker, a fishmonger and the harbormaster. A large wooden pier jutted out into the harbor. There were only a couple of small boats at anchor in the bay. Eric guessed the fishermen were out at sea.

The gray water lapped against the stone of the harbor wall with a gentle slap, slap. The sea breeze brought a sharp salt tang to Eric's nostrils. He could hear the cries of the seagulls that flew overhead.

"Can you understand what they're saying?" he asked Stig.

"Rude creatures," Stig snorted. "They're making fun of my ancestry."

Eric and Kate laughed. Eric scanned the bay and saw the two ridges that formed the harbor reaching out like arms to embrace it. Palm trees grew on the top of each ridge, their long, slender leaves blowing like hair in the breeze. Eric's eyes narrowed.

"The entrance to the harbor is pretty narrow," he said.

"Only about three of our fishing boats can sail through it side by side," Kate said. "And the pirate ships are so big, they have to sail single file into the harbor."

Beyond the bay, the sun was setting into the sea. The sky became a bright orange that changed to pink, then rose, and finally purple as the sun sank lower and lower.

Eric surveyed the beautiful scene and was surprised to find himself outlining the beginnings of a plan. "Well, I guess it's a start," he murmured.

"What was that?" Stig asked.

"Uh, nothing. C'mon," Eric turned to walk back up the hill. "It's probably time for dinner."

The more he thought about his idea as they walked, the more excited he became. It might just work, he thought as they reached the house. I just wish I knew what I was doing.

CHAPTER 4

COUNCIL

Eric had felt a rising feeling of panic at dinner that night when the Lord Mayor had told Eric and Kate that they were to address the Council. Naturally, the news made Kate bubble with excitement. "I can't believe it! Going to a Council! Just think. We're the youngest people ever to speak! They'll want me to tell them everything about finding you, and you'll explain your plan to defeat the pirates. Wow, what an honor!"

Kate's constant chatter annoyed Eric. She was so sure of herself, while he had no idea—none—what he was going to say. The plan he had thought halfway decent earlier didn't look too good to him now as he walked, stomach churning, while Kate talked nonstop all the way across the Green. Eric fought a growing urge to tell her to shut up.

"Very few women ever attend Council meetings," she was saying. "And it was only about twenty years ago that women were allowed to be elected, and then only three out of nine. Even worse, the eldest *son* of the Endria family inherits the title of Lord Mayor. That's not fair, is it?"

"What?" Eric hadn't really been paying attention.

"I should be Lord Mayor after Papa retires, but since I'm a girl, that can't happen."

"That's pretty lame," Eric snorted. "What kind of backward village is this?"

"Perhaps not so backward that we can't change," the Lord Mayor said with a slight smile. "I've been pushing for Calendria to accept Kate as my eventual successor, but many are reluctant to accept such a radical concept."

"Will the whole village be there tonight?" Eric felt his forehead getting damp, even though the evening was cool.

"No," Kate said, "just the Council. They'll listen to my story, then they'll listen to your plan and decide what to do."

"Yeah, my plan." Eric's stomach churned faster, and his knees felt weak. "Do I have to come up with a whole plan?"

"That's why you were sent, isn't it?" Kate asked.

Eric felt the Lord Mayor's eyes on him as they walked.

"Oh sure, yeah, that's what I thought." He felt like he was going to puke. "I was just making sure is all. Uh, but what if the Council doesn't believe that Stig and I are here to help?" Stig had been strangely silent since dinner. He's got the easy job this mission, letting the new guy do all the work, Eric thought.

"Papa will convince them." Kate sounded absolutely certain. "They'll probably hear the facts, ask some questions and then vote on it."

The meeting hall didn't look half as amazing to Eric as Kate's house. It was a square brick building with wide wooden stairs that led to a white door with windows on either side. The Lord Mayor ushered them into the council chamber, a large room with a polished wooden table and twelve chairs as the only furniture. A huge chandelier, with dozens of candles, hung from the vaulted ceiling directly overhead, filling the room with a flickering light.

On the wall, Eric spotted a round plaque divided into quarters depicting a boat, a plow, an anvil and an eagle. The motto "Calendria, Peace, Freedom, Justice," ran around the outer edge.

The Lord Mayor took his place at the head of the table and motioned Eric to sit on his left, Kate on his right. Stig perched on the table between Eric and the Lord Mayor. They'd just settled down when the door opened with a squeak and the Council filed in. Eric watched as each checked out him and Stig, trying not to stare too hard. He wondered how much the Lord Mayor had told them.

The Lord Mayor rose and made introductions all around. The Council comprised nine villagers. Cordon was the town blacksmith. He was a burly, dark-skinned man with a bushy beard and long, dark hair tied in a ponytail. His brown eyes bored into Eric, who thought he looked quite fierce. Moira Bottleneck, the apothecary, looked at Eric and Stig through a pair of wire-rimmed glasses and gave them both a slight smile. The harbormaster, Captain Weatherbee, was a weather-beaten middle-aged man. Nan Stitch, the net mender, was younger and had a feisty look. The other Council members were two older farmers, Jasper Twigg and Dan Furrow; the stonemason, Mr. Flint; the cooper, a round woman named Mrs. Casker; and a woodworker by the name of Chip Wainscott, who Eric thought looked to be in his early twenties. When the introductions had been made, the Lord Mayor addressed the Council.

"My fellow Council members," he said, "thank you for coming on such short notice. What I have to discuss with you is very important, and I thought it best to meet with you as quickly as possible. As you know, ever since the pirates broke faith with us more than two hundred years ago, we have been subject to their unjust tariff. While we've chafed under their yoke, we haven't been bold enough to put a stop to it. We've dreamed of the time when we will, even had a legend—the Deliverers—spring up about that day, but we've never taken action.

"I've called this Council because I believe that the time has finally come to defy Sharky and his crew."

There was a great deal of muttering among the Council. Cordon the blacksmith rose. His shrewd brown eyes met the Lord Mayor's. "Your Honor, what makes you think that this is the proper time? Why now?"

"A good question, Cordon," the Mayor frowned. "One that I'm not rightly sure I can answer. The Deliverers legend is just that—legend. It tells of two heroes, a man and an eagle with the gift of speech, who appear suddenly to liberate Calendria.

"Some of us believe the legend to be literal, that the two heroes will appear exactly as in the legend. My daughter, Kate, is one of these." Kate nodded. "Others believe that the legend is allegorical—that events will follow the general theme of the legend and lead us to liberty. Still others put no stock in the legend at all"—here Cordon snorted—"saying that it's too farfetched, that we must save ourselves if we're to be saved at all.

"For my own part, I believe that there is some truth to the legend. Strangers may come and either rouse us or perhaps actually help us overthrow Sharky and his crew.

"My daughter, in her youthful fancy, spends a great deal of time patrolling the beach and searching for the Deliverers. She is young and sees it as part of her duty to Calendria. As for me, I see no harm in indulging her in this."

"Bunch of foolishness if you ask me," Cordon muttered. "That's just a taste of what it'll be like if we ever have a woman in charge."

"That's enough of that," the Lord Mayor snapped. "You will have your chance to speak, Cordon, you know the protocol."

"My pardon, your honor." Cordon hung his head. "I forgot myself and spoke out of turn."

"As I said, my daughter, Kate, searches almost daily and always comes back empty-handed. That is, until today."

The council members began to murmur, sounding, Eric thought, like a swarm of bees.

The Lord Mayor raised his hands in a quieting gesture. "Order, please. Today, she turned up with this young man and a strange bird, one that's not native to our land, called an owl. I have asked my daughter and the two strangers to appear before you and tell you what has transpired so far."

There was more buzzing as the Mayor sat and Kate stood to address the Council. "Greetings, council members. I thank you for the opportunity to address you," she said. It seemed to Eric that she was repeating some sort of traditional greeting. "As most of you know, I have been searching for the Deliverers since my mother died. She had a very strong belief in the legend, and she passed that on to me.

"Today, I was walking through the jungle, heading to the beach beyond the eastern ridge. I always search the beach because I've always thought the Deliverers would come from over the sea. Just before I reached the end of the jungle, I saw a boy on the beach through the trees."

And with that, she recounted the story of their meeting on the beach and all that followed. When she had finished, the murmur had become a roar. Cordon jumped to his feet and thumped the table with a huge callused hand. "Impossible! How could a bird talk? Even if there were some truth to the legend, and I've never thought so, how could these be the Deliverers? That bird is no eagle and," he pointed at Eric, "he's no hero, just a boy. What good can they do? It's ridiculous!"

Nan the net mender nodded and looked at the Mayor. "It does seem rather farfetched, your Honor. I don't see what help a boy can possibly be. As for the bird, even if he *can* talk, he's not an eagle."

Eric was beginning to get angry. He and Stig were here to help and, although that didn't seem likely to him, they weren't even being given a chance. Without thinking, he jumped to his feet.

"Hey!" he yelled above the confusion. The room became silent. All eyes turned to him. He began to sweat, wishing he'd kept his mouth shut. "Uh, I know we aren't what you expected, but we're here for a reason. If you don't want our help, well, that's up to you; this whole place seems kinda backward to me anyway. You might actually want to keep paying this Tariff, for all I know. You must, since you haven't done anything about it. I know you're all afraid of the pirates and their cannon, but where I'm from, we have things that are much worse. Still, it's a tough problem, and who knows what will happen if you try to stop this Sharky dude and fail. I mean, he is like a thousand years old, so he's probably a lot smarter than you. I just think that you have to try. If you're not free, what's the point?"

Stig cleared his throat. "My young friend is right. You're not free; you're just Sharky's slaves. To win your freedom, you'll have to risk everything. We can't make that decision for you, of course; you have to do that on your own. If that's what you decide, then we will help in any way possible."

The council members turned and stared at the owl. Some opened their mouths in a silent question, and then closed them again.

The Mayor rose to his feet. "The fact of the matter, my friends, is the bird *can* talk, and that alone gives the legend credence. Eric is right, as well. We have to overcome our fear and fight. I say we look very closely at this matter and form a council of war to develop a plan to overthrow the pirates. The time has come, my friends, when we must risk all, and we haven't a moment to lose."

"I agree that something must be done," Mrs. Casker said. Her plump face was crinkled in a frown. "But the question is, what?"

"I've been havin' my lads makin' extra weapons for a couple of years, now," said Cordon. "We've managed to stow away enough cutlasses and axes and bows and arrows to arm most of the village. When Sharky comes ashore, we can surround him and force the others to lay down their arms."

"That'll never work, Cordon," Farmer Twigg shook his gray head. "They'll just lay into us with their cannon. You know Sharky has standing orders to fire if we ever make a move, no matter what danger he's in himself."

"I agree," said the Mayor. "It's too risky without a proper plan. I know you went to a lot of trouble and personal risk to make those weapons, Cordon, but without a plan, all your work will be in vain."

"Lord Mayor, may I make a suggestion?" Moira Bottleneck asked.

"Please, Moira," replied the Lord Mayor, "go right ahead."

"It seems to me that, if young master Eric and his friend Stig *are* the Deliverers, then it is their task to devise a plan to defeat Sharky and his band of cutthroats and our job to do whatever is in our power to assist them."

There was a murmur of agreement from the rest of the Council.

Eric, who had come to the same conclusion earlier that day and was hoping he was wrong, noticed the queasy feeling growing in his stomach again. He leaned over to Stig and whispered, "Well, that's done it."

"It's why you were chosen for this Assignment," the owl whispered back. "Like it or not, it's what you're supposed to do."

"Thanks a lot," Eric replied. "You're a big help. I have a couple of ideas, but it's not really a plan."

"Well, it's bound to be better than anything anyone's said so far," Stig said.

The Lord Mayor held his hands up for silence. "That's a big task for one so young, Moira."

But Kate was tugging at her father's sleeve. "He can do it, Papa. They both can. They're the Deliverers. It's their job."

Eric didn't think the Lord Mayor looked so sure, but the look of supreme confidence Kate was giving him and Stig didn't make him feel any less nervous. Eric returned her look and stood. "Uh, Lord Mayor, can I ask a few questions?"

The Lord Mayor turned and regarded Eric with his deep brown eyes. He nodded. "The floor is yours, lad, if you're up to it."

"Um, thanks. Uh, hello, members of the Council," Eric began. "I, uh, have some ideas." He paused, and the Council quieted, waiting for him to continue. "I've been thinking. Kate took us on a tour of the harbor this afternoon, and I, um, just wanted to get some other information from you."

"Go ahead, young fella, ask away," Captain Weatherbee said.

"Well, ah, how many ships does Captain Sharky bring on Tariff Day?"

"Three, lad," Captain Weatherbee said. "His flagship, *Death-wind*, and two smaller ships."

"And Kate says they have to sail into the harbor single file, right?"

"Aye, that's right."

"Do they sail bunched together?"

"No, matter of fact, they're a little sloppy. Sail in all loose-like," replied the Captain. "I guess they reckon we're not going to put up much of a fuss."

Eric nodded, and thought his idea could work. "Uh, Lord Mayor, how long is it until the next Tariff Day?"

"Well, it's late July now, and the next tariff is the beginning of October, so we've a little more than two months to prepare."

It seemed to Eric to be enough time, but he wasn't sure. "Well, uh, this is my plan. It's got some holes, but I hope we can fill them in as we go along. We have to have something to bargain with, which means we have to, uh, capture Captain Sharky."

"How're ya gonna do that, lad?" Cordon asked. "We're no match for three warships armed with cannon."

"Well, uh, the pirates are gonna do some damage to the village; I don't think we can avoid that," Eric admitted. "But if everything goes right, we'll keep them from doing too much damage by trapping Sharky in the harbor and keeping the other two ships out."

"How?" Cordon asked.

Here goes nothing, Eric thought, hope they don't laugh too hard. "Well, I was thinking we could make a large net and submerge it at the harbor mouth. When Sharky's flagship sails through, we could raise the net with block and tackle set up on the two ridges overlooking the entrance to the harbor and block the other two ships out."

"What's to keep them ships from blasting their way through?" Captain Weatherbee asked.

"We could put a couple of catapults on the ridges—would we have enough time to make them, Cordon?"

The blacksmith nodded. "Chip and I've been toyin' with makin' a few. We've made a few models, actually. Never made any, though— didn't know where we could hide 'em."

"Okay, cool. So we could fire the catapults at them. Try to sink them, but mainly just distract 'em, slow 'em down a little. But we don't *have* to sink 'em, just keep 'em occupied until we can capture Sharky."

Everyone stared at Eric. He felt the sweat trickle down his back.

"Uh, what's the matter?" he asked.

"I think they're a bit fuzzy on the capture Sharky part," Stig whispered. "To be honest with you, I must admit that I am as well."

"The whole idea of the plan is to capture Captain Sharky and the crew of his flagship," Eric said.

"I think we understand the general idea," Cordon said. "But how do we do that? What's to stop Sharky's flagship from blasting the village and then blasting its way out of the harbor?"

"Um, well, about a third of the way inside the harbor, we string an iron chain about six or seven feet below the waterline. I read about it in a book once: the chain'll have iron spikes about five feet long every few feet along its length, all pointing toward the mouth of the harbor. Before they see it, they'll ram into it. It'll happen so fast, they won't have time to turn around, and the ship will be impaled and probably sink. We'll take Cordon's weapons and row out to fish Sharky and his crew out of the water. Uh, how does that sound?"

"It's a little rough around the edges," the Lord Mayor said.

"That chain's going to take some time; it'll be close," Cordon said. "But if I put some extra folk on the job, we could do it, I think. Then we'll stick it to old Sharky!" The big man grinned.

The other members of the Council were grinning as well. Kate raced from her chair and gave Eric a hug. He felt his face burning. Stig nodded his approval.

"Not bad for a beginner," he said.

"Really?" Eric asked.

Cordon beckoned to the boy from his seat at the far end of the conference table. "Why don't you come down here, lad, and tell Chip and me more about that chain and the block-and-tackle device. How big do you reckon they'll have to be?"

The Council lasted far into the night. Eric's plan was refined and logistics hammered out. Captain Weatherbee proved to be an invaluable asset in that regard. His knowledge of the harbor—its depths, dimensions—was encyclopedic. By the time Eric got to bed, it was way past midnight. He couldn't help but feel a little smug. He'd actually come up with a plan, and the Council had accepted it. Not a bad first day's work he thought as he dropped off to sleep.

CHAPTER 5

RESCUE

The next day, the work began in earnest. Eric spent many hours with Cordon the blacksmith, Chip Wainscott the woodworker, and the other Council members over the next week, helping with the planning and preparation. Stig spent hours doing aerial reconnaissance of the harbor and village and flew messages from one area to another.

Late one morning, after another meeting with the Lord Mayor, Cordon and Chip, Eric ran to find Kate and Stig. They were sitting at the base of Cal Endria's statue, which stood in the center of the Green. Kate was recounting a bit of her ancestor's history for Stig.

"Calvin Endria was a great explorer. Not only did he discover the harbor that became Calendria, but he searched for a path over the Iron Mountains," Kate was saying as Eric ran up. "He thought that one day the village could relocate on the other side, away from Sharky."

"You don't say," Stig said. "I gather he never found a way across?"

"If he did, he didn't get a chance to tell anyone about it. He was lost in the mountains. He made a total of four journeys. After the third, he told his son that he'd decided to take another approach, that he'd found a guide or something."

"You mean a map?" Eric puffed, still breathing hard.

Kate frowned. "It could have been; the tales aren't very clear."

"Perhaps it was someone from beyond the mountains," Stig suggested.

"I doubt it. That would have been big news. I can't see how it could be hushed up," Kate said.

"Maybe he found a path or a marker, something like that," Eric said.

Kate shrugged. "Whatever it was, Cal Endria set off on his fourth and final journey alone and never returned. The path he took ended at a sheer cliff face. No one ever found a trace of him."

"Kate, Cordon's been telling me about the iron mine," Eric said. "It sounds cool. How about going up to check it out?"

"Okay," Kate said. "The mine's at the base of the mountains. It's going to be busy, though; they're working like crazy now."

They set off along a small road that wound behind the grounds of the mayor's house toward the mountains. After hiking a little less than a mile through a strip of forest, they came out at the foothills of the mountain range. Kate and Eric followed the road, which led between two hills, while Stig flew above them. After passing through the little valley, they came to the mine.

It was dug into the side of the largest mountain Eric had ever seen. The entrance was braced with timbers, and men were coming in and out in a steady ebb and flow. Some were pushing carts full of iron ore; others were carrying tools and lanterns. Everyone looked very busy.

"They're really working hard," Eric said.

"Quite so," Stig agreed. "It doesn't appear that they have any time to spare to give two children and an owl a tour."

"Well, we have to do something," Kate said. "We've come all the way out here, and it's barely noon."

Eric studied the mountains with a thoughtful look. I wonder, he thought. Kate noticed his look. "You've got an idea?"

Eric nodded. "Yeah, why don't we explore the mountains a little? Who knows? We might find Cal Endria's path."

"Or his guide." Kate grinned.

"Yeah, his guide." Eric smiled.

"Now wait a minute, youngsters," Stig fluttered down onto a boulder and held up his wings in a cautioning gesture. "Don't think for a minute that I'm going to be part of some wild scheme to find a route over those mountains."

"We're not going to go over," Eric said. "We're just going to see if we can find any trace of Cal Endria's guide. Kate, do you know where he began his final journey?"

"Oh sure, there's a marker at the beginning of the trail. It's a village landmark. Like I said, though, it leads to a dead end. I've been there before. It's not far, I'll show you."

"Now see here. I must insist that we head back to the village this instant," Stig demanded. "We've got trouble enough as it is without a jaunt in the mountains."

"Oh, come on, Stig," Kate said. "The adults are doing very nicely now that you and Eric have gotten them started. They'll be all right without us getting underfoot for an afternoon. We're actually doing them a favor."

"Yeah," Eric said. "They'll probably thank us for staying out of the way. Come on, where's your sense of adventure?"

"Being strangled by my common sense," the owl muttered, but he flew into the air and followed them.

57

Kate led them past the mine along a grassy track. A half-hour later, they stood before a plain pillar of stone about five feet high with a small ball set on top. It stood beside a dirt path that led up into the mountains. Words were engraved on the marker. Eric read it aloud.

"Here, in 30 AF (After Founding),
began the final journey of our founder, Calvin Endria.
He departed in search of a passage through
these mountains and never returned.
I, Lord Mayor Colin Endria, and all the people of Calendria,
have set this marker here as a memorial
to Calvin Endria in the year 35 AF.
We shall forever be in his debt."

Eric looked up the steep and winding path. A wave of excitement swept over him. "So, let's get going. We'll have to hurry if we want to get back by dark."

"Not if we run," Kate said, and dashed up the path, disappearing around a bend.

"Hey, wait up," Eric said, and ran after her.

Stig flew after them. "Wait!" he cried. "We must all stay together!"

Eric didn't pay any attention. His only thought as he raced up the path was to catch Kate. Mountain walls loomed on either side of him, sheer and tall. An occasional ledge or rock outcropping jutted out over the trail. Puffing, he finally caught Kate, and grabbed her arm. She spun to face him, laughing.

"Caught you!" he said.

"Took you long enough," Kate retorted. "You wouldn't have gotten half as far if *I* had been chasing *you*."

"Sure, right," Eric laughed. "I'd have been all the way up the path by now."

Just then, Stig arrived. He landed, scowling, on a large rock by the side of the path. "I might have known you two would start behaving like children eventually," he said. "What do you mean, running headlong into unexplored territory like that? There could be anything up here. Why don't you use some common sense? You're both intelligent children—for humans."

"Hey, don't worry about it," Eric said. He thought Stig acted too much like a grown-up, and for some reason that annoyed him. "You're not my father, you know. Just because you're like a thousand years old, that doesn't mean we have to be boring, too."

"Yeah," Kate said. "Loosen up, Stig. This isn't unexplored territory. I've been here a bunch of times."

"All right," Stig shrugged. "Suit yourselves. Do whatever you want. You seem to know best. After all, I've never done this type of thing more than a dozen times. I obviously don't know what I'm talking about. Well, let's go. Perhaps we can all find a nice cliff to jump from."

"Oh, Stig, calm down," Kate said. "Of course we should be careful, but there's nothing to worry about here. Trust me. We're almost to the end, anyway."

"I don't know how I got stuck with two such impertinent children," Stig grumbled. "I'm sure I don't know what I've done to deserve this. All right, we're here, so we might as well continue. But do be sensible. Stay close and keep your voices down so the whole mountain doesn't know we're coming."

They continued on, a little more slowly and quietly to please the owl. After rounding another couple of bends, they came to a dead end. The path ended in a wall of solid rock that rose high into the air. An outcrop of rock jutted out from it about 25 feet overhead.

Eric looked at the wall and whistled. "Wow, that's some cliff. You say there was no sign of Cal Endria when the village searched for him?"

"None," Kate said. "It's our biggest mystery. In fact..."

She was cut off by a high wail that echoed off the mountain walls. Startled, Eric looked up. He saw a little man hanging by his hands from the ledge above them. His red beard hung straight down, while his short legs flailed about.

"Help! Help!" he wailed.

Kate looked at Eric, who shrugged and then cupped his hands to his mouth. "Don't worry," he called. "We'll get you down!" Eric reached in his backpack and took out a coil of nylon rope. He shook it out and said, "Stig, fly up to the ledge and wrap the end of my rope around one of those rocks up there." He put one end of the rope in the owl's beak, and Stig flew it up to the ledge and wrapped the rope around a large rock.

"Grab the rope and climb down!" Eric yelled.

The little man reached a trembling hand out for the rope, but couldn't quite reach it.

"Stretch a little," Eric called.

"I don't think I can," he groaned.

Eric's stomach felt like lead. Oh man, he thought, if he keeps shaking like that, he's gonna fall. Visions of his father falling flashed through his mind.

"I'll see what I can do," Stig called. The owl flew from the ledge, grabbed the middle of the rope in his beak, and brought it within reach of the man, who took hold and began to climb down.

"Kate, do you know who he is?" Eric asked as he watched the little man inching down the rope.

60

"I've never seen him before," she said, shaking her head. "No one I know of in Calendria is that short, besides a child, I mean."

The little man reached the ground and stood before them, bowing low. Although only about three and a half feet tall, Eric saw that he was powerfully built. His hair, beard and shaggy eyebrows were a flaming red, and his blue eyes were bright. He wore a plaid shirt that reminded Eric of those worn by lumberjacks, and blue pants held up by green suspenders. His black boots were shabby-looking and unpolished. Eric realized he was a dwarf.

"I'm right grateful to ya for helpin' me. I was in a tight fix an' no mistake," the dwarf said, dusting himself off. Then he stopped and peered at them. "Well now, what manner o' folk are ya?"

"Us?" Kate asked. "We're people, just like you."

"Ya mean Big Folk?" The dwarf peered at them even closer. "Where're your beards?"

"We don't have beards," Eric said. How dumb was this guy? "I'm too young and Kate's a girl; girls don't have beards."

"Well I heard Big Folk was a queer lot," the dwarf said. He scratched his beard. "All dwarves has whiskers from the time they're little 'uns. Me mammy, may she rest in peace, had a thick golden beard, talk o' the Kingdom it were. She were right beautiful, don't ya know."

Eric and Kate looked at each other.

"Mark m' words, lassie, work on growin' a beard. Ya won't never regret it."

"Er, um, thanks. I'll think about it," Kate promised. "What were you doing up on the ledge?"

"Well, lassie, I guess ya could say I was dyin', but had a change o' heart."

"I don't get it." She frowned.

61

"Well, I had made up m' mind t' throw m'self off that cliff, don't ya know, but halfway inta doin' it, I changed m' mind and decided not t' do it." His face crinkled into a wry grin. "But by that time it were too late—I'd a jumped clean over the edge. Fortunately dwarves have very strong hands, an' I were able t' grab the ledge with one o' 'em. That's about when you young 'uns an' this very helpful bird showed up."

"Why were you jumping off the cliff?" Eric asked.

"Well now, laddie, that's a story an' a half an' no mistake. I s'pose I should start with m' name, which, it just so happens, is part o' the problem. M' name is Hallo, Hallo Tosis, a cruel joke on the part o' m' pappy, who has a nasty sense o' humor. So ya see, I was startin' off with one hand tied behind m' back from the get-go. M' people live under these mountains, don't ya know, which is perfect 'cause it don't encourage visitors, an' we're a private folk.

"We like t' delve in the mountains minin' metals an' buildin' huge caverns o' stone in which we live. M' people're wonderful crafts-men an' have a talent for metal an' stone work. Everyone, that is, 'cept yours truly. I ain't got no talent for it, don't ya know—the only one o' m' kind without the Gift, as we call it.

"M' pappy were devastated, as ya kin well imagine. He's the Roy-al Goldsmithy, a right important position, don't ya know, an' I made him a laughin' stock. Everyone in the Kingdom never let 'im forget what a failure I were. 'Course m' name didn't help none. Finally, after more'n a century o' study with the best smithys and stonemasons— all o' which wrote me off as hopeless—m' pappy turned me out o' his house. He's tight with the King, so he were able t' get me banished. Now I'm an outcast, forced t' wander the mountains trying t' scrape together enough t' keep body an' soul together. I've been a wanderin' for over a year.

"I scratched out a small hole in a cliff t' live in, but the ceilin' kept cavin' in, don't ya know. I kept wakin' up in the middle o' the night covered in rocks an' dirt, thinkin' I were dead an' buried. Finally, I took t' sleepin' outdoors, but if I weren't gettin' rained on, I was bein' trod on in the dark by varmints.

"Just now, I'd decided that enough were enough. I clumb up t' that ledge an' jumped. Then, like I says, I done changed m' mind in mid-leap, don't ya know, an' made a grab. Then you come along, an' here we are."

"I say, that's some story," Stig said. "Well, old boy, chin up. I was rather different from the others in my flock as well, and I've landed on my talons. I daresay things will work out the same for you in the end."

The dwarf's jaw dropped. "Now don't that beat all. I thought he were just trained, but it seems he's a right peculiar bird all right. M' folks always said the Big Folk were a odd lot, beggin' your pardon an' all. I guess they wasn't lyin'."

Eric's brow furrowed. He had an idea. "Listen, Hallo—is it okay to call you Hallo?"

"Don't see why not." The dwarf shrugged. "It's better than m' full name, an' plain Tosis ain't so hot, neither."

"How would you like to come back to Calendria with us?" Eric asked.

"What, an' live with Big Folk?" Hallo scratched his beard. "I don't rightly know. It ain't been done afore that I know of. It just don't seem natural t' me somehow."

"Calendria's in trouble, and you look like a strong, able-bodied person," Eric said. "So I thought you might be willing to help us. You'd get three good meals a day and a roof over your head."

Hallo frowned. "Dwarves prefer four meals, an' what's the use o' a roof over a body's head if'n the pirates come along an' blow it off, along with m' head t' boot?"

Kate's eyes widened in surprise. "You know about the pirates?"

"Ah, lassie, why shouldn't I?" Hallo asked. "I've had the best seat in the house t' watch 'em, don't ya know. Every six months they come, sometimes fire some black powder at a shed or two, and then ya grovel an' give 'em anythin' they want."

"Well, what do you expect us to do?" Kate demanded, hands on hips.

"Why don't ya fire some black powder back at 'em?" Hallo replied. "Give 'em as good as ya get, I say!"

"Because," Kate said through gritted teeth. "We don't know how to make it."

"Not know how t' make black powder?" Hallo scoffed. "Even I know how t' make it. We use it for tunnelin'. It's one o' our oldest, most usefulest tools, don't ya know. Imagine not bein' able t' make black powder. Don't ya have an apothecary down there?"

"We do." Kate drew herself up. "As a matter of fact, she's very wise, and a master of her art. Papa says there's none better."

"Can't be so hot if she don't know how t' make a simple thing like black powder," Hallo muttered.

Kate's voice went up an octave. "Madame Bottleneck is a very wise woman. She knows a lot more than some people I could mention."

The dwarf's face turned as red as his beard. "Listen, lassie, no child's gonna talk t' me that way! Where I'm from, wise-talkin' children get a spankin'."

"Calm down, you two," Eric broke in. "Don't argue. Kate, once he meets her, I'm sure Hallo will see that Madame Bottleneck is a great apothecary, and Hallo, I'm sure she'd like to learn about the ancient craft of the dwarves."

Kate studied the mountaintops while Hallo gazed at the ground and kicked a small stone in the dust.

"I guess that, mebbe, I were a bit hasty," Hallo allowed. Your Madame Bottleneck is most likely a very fine apothecary for all I know. 'Sides, I ain't got no call t' be speakin' t' ya'll that way, bein' how ya saved m' life an' all. I'm deep in your debt an' right grateful. If ya think I can be o' some service in your fight against them pirates then I'll be proud t' help ya." He extended a strong crooked hand to Kate, who smiled and grabbed it with both of hers.

"I'm sorry, too, Hallo," she said. "Of course, we could really use your help. This is wonderful. Sharky and his men will get a real shock when they realize we're firing cannon right back at them!"

"Well, now that everything's settled, why don't we head back to the village? I daresay your father will want to be informed of this development straightaway," Stig said, and launched himself into the air.

The children and the dwarf followed the owl back down the trail. Eric caught hold of Hallo's sleeve and slowed him down until they were out of earshot of Kate, who was talking with Stig as they went.

"Hallo," he said, "Can you really teach the villagers how to make black powder?"

The dwarf's face broke into a grin. "Oh sure, lad. No problem, it's as easy as fallin' off a log, don't ya know. Any ninny could do it."

"Really?" Eric pressed. Somehow, he had his doubts.

"Sure, it ain't nothin', er, that's what me pappy always said." Hallo fidgeted a bit.

"What's that supposed to mean?" Eric stopped and stared hard at the dwarf.

"Well, it's just that, uh, I know the ingredients, but I have a little trouble blendin' 'em."

"A little trouble?"

"Yeah, I ain't ever gotten it t' work just right. Ya might say it usually blows up in m' face, don't ya know." The dwarf grinned.

"Blows up?" Eric had a terrible vision of Calendria being blown sky high.

"I wouldn't worry, though, laddie," Hallo said. "I'm sure that Madame Bubblebeak or whatever her name is'll do a fair piece better'n me. I'll give her the ingredients, and she'll be able t' whip up a batch in no time, I'm sure, from what the lass says."

He gave the boy another huge smile and rushed to catch up with the others on his sturdy little legs. Eric continued to lag behind, troubled by his thoughts. When Hallo had said he knew the recipe for black powder, Eric had been just as excited as the others, thinking that victory was assured. Now he wasn't so sure. He hoped the apothecary was as good as Kate claimed, but something told him it wasn't going to be as easy as it seemed to come up with the right mixture.

That wasn't the only thing that was bothering him, however. There was something tugging at the back of his mind. As the little group made its way down the path, he had the inexplicable feeling that they should be going back up.

CHAPTER 6

SHARKY

Captain Burt Sharky glared at the trembling pirate who stood before him. His left hand fidgeted with a ring on his right hand. The jagged red stone set in the ring glowed with a blood-red light. He was seated in a high-backed chair in the middle of his audience chamber, a gloomy hall where the pirate captain held court while at his island base.

Sharky was six and a half feet tall. He wore breeches and black boots that came up to his knees. A red frock coat covered a yellowed linen shirt. His head was covered by a blue and yellow bandana from under which jutted shocks of fiery red hair. His eyes were a piercing green, and the beard on his scarred face was as red as his hair.

"Repeat that, Fishbane," he snarled. "I don't think I heard ye aright."

"Well, Cap'n," Fishbane twisted the hat he held in his trembling hands, "me an' a few o' the lads went t' scout the village, same as we always does. We landed on the beach t' the south an' climbed up t' the top o' the ridge.

"Things was bustlin' there, but it didn't seem like the usual goin's on."

"Aye, ye said that afore, Fishbane," Sharky growled. "But what were differ'nt about it?"

"Well, sir, there were a lot more comin' an' goin' from the iron mine fer one thing. An' a bunch o' farmers was clearin' trees and such from the two ridges above the harbor mouth, an' they was buildin' stone walls up there. The net mender an' a group o' others was weavin' a 'uge net. An' later on, I saw her an' a group of villagers in the jungle practicin' arch'ry."

"Archery, anythin' else?" Sharky spat.

Fishbane's ruddy face twisted in concentration, then he brightened. "Oh yeah, I almost fergot. I waited 'til night and snuck down to the blacksmith's. I looked in the winder and, they're forgin' weapons!"

"Yer sure of that?" Sharky twisted the ring on his finger.

"Aye, Cap'n, it were just like I said."

"All right, Fishbane, that's all. Ye done good. Go get yerself some grub."

"Thank'ee, sir," Fishbane made an awkward bow, turned and fled.

"Marrow!" Sharky bellowed.

Out of the shadows came a thin figure. He ambled over to the captain's chair without a trace of fear. Cruel eyes stared out of an emaciated head, which looked like a skull. He was Sharky's first mate, and the men were almost as afraid of him as they were of the Captain.

"You called, Captain?" Mr. Marrow's voice was cool as ice.

"Ye heard that weasel's report?"

"Aye, sir."

"The swine're up t' somethin'," Sharky grumbled.

"Undoubtedly, Captain," Mr. Marrow agreed.

"I'm a-thinkin' they're fixin' on settin' a trap," Sharky played with his ring.

"Perhaps the sheep seek to become wolves," Mr. Marrow's eyes held an icy gleam.

"They wouldn't dare!" Sharky bellowed, slamming his fist down on the arm of his chair. "They ain't never been no trouble afore! Who could o' stirred 'em up?"

"Well, that blacksmith, Cordon, he's always been belligerent, and then there's the Lord Mayor himself," Mr. Marrow suggested.

"Oh ho!" Sharky barked. "Them Endrias 'ave always been sheep. They've no stomach fer fightin', never 'ave, never will. And that goes fer the rest o' 'em. They dance t' Endria's tune, they does. It ain't never gonna change."

Mr. Marrow's eyes narrowed, and he cocked his head to one side. "Hmmm, Charles Endria may be made of sterner stuff than you give him credit for. His family has always been independent."

Sharky scowled. "Don't be daft, man. He's a sheep--they're all sheep I tell ye!"

"And yet it seems they're setting a trap for us at the next Tariff," Mr. Marrow pursed thin lips.

"Aye, so it seems." Sharky's eyes narrowed, and a cruel smile curled his lip. "But they don't know we're on to 'em, eh, Marrow? They may be playin' at bein' wolves, but in the end, sheep they'll be. They'll turn tail an' run."

"And if they aren't just sheep?" Mr. Marrow asked.

"Then we'll wipe 'em out," Sharky hissed.

CHAPTER 7

OLD TALES

Madame Bottleneck frowned at the list she held in her hands. "Anyone who mixed these ingredients according to the directions would blow themselves up," she said.

"I know, ma'am," Hallo said. "I've proven that a few times m'self."

"Still," the apothecary's eyes narrowed behind her small wire-rimmed glasses. "This is an interesting list. I may be able to develop a formula for black powder with these directions, but it will take time."

"How much time, Moira?" the Lord Mayor asked.

Madame Bottleneck brushed aside a wisp of gray hair that had fallen into her eyes. "I'm not sure, Charles. My apprentices and I will have to work carefully. It's extremely dangerous. One mistake and boom!" She smacked her hands together.

"I realize you'll have to go cautiously, Moira, but do you think you'll have the solution in time for Tariff Day?"

"Hmmm," the apothecary pursed her lips. "I'm not sure, but we'll do our best. Now, I think it's time you all cleared out of here. I've got a lot of work to do."

"Keep me updated on your progress, Moira," the Lord Mayor said.

"If my shop doesn't blow up, that means things are going well. If it does, that means I've botched it," she laughed. "Now shoo!"

They exited the shop, and the Lord Mayor left them to get back to work. Eric and his friends headed over to the statue of Cal Endria, their unofficial gathering place during their rare time off. As the two children flopped down at the base of the statue and Stig landed on the grass beside them, Hallo gazed up at Cal Endria's stone face.

"Ya know, he looks just like m' pappy describes him," he said.

"What do you mean?" Kate sat up straight.

"Ya mean t' tell me ya don't know?" Hallo took off his cap and scratched his head.

"Know what?" Kate asked. "Hallo, if you know something about Cal Endria, you better tell me."

"Well," Hallo put his cap back on and spread his hands. "It's just that I thought ya'd know 'bout his journey through the Kingdom."

"Hallo," Eric said slowly. "Cal Endria went through the Dwarf Kingdom looking for a route under the mountains?"

"Yeah, he did, leastways that's what m' pappy says. I weren't borned yet, don't ya know—I'm only 197. But Pap says that this here Cal Endria," Hallo pointed at the statue, "what founded this here village tried t' go over the mountains a few times, which if ya ask me is kind o' daft, seein' as you'd have t' be a eagle t' do it.

"Anyway, on one trip he met up with a young dwarf who fer some reason, m' pappy wouldn't say why, agreed t' guide him under the mountains. The dwarf told ol' Endria 'bout the Kingdom an' 'bout the Forbidden Door what opens t' the other side o' the mountains."

"Wait a minute," Kate said. "There's a route under the mountains to the other side?"

Hallo nodded. "I guess ol' Endria got real excited an' begged the dwarf t' take him t' the king t' get his permission. For some reason, the dwarf said okay an' took him t' see King Rufus Thunderhelm, for the okay t' pass through the Kingdom. Pap says that Endria were a brave man, an' he'd've had ta been t' want t' go through the Forbidden Door. Well, the king give his okay, but he told Endria he had t' go alone, 'cause the king didn't want t' put any o' his subjects inta danger, don't ya know."

"What happened to Cal Endria?" Kate's eyes were intent.

"King Rufus opened the Forbidden Door. Endria went through, an' he were gone. That were the last anyone ever saw o' him," Hallo shrugged.

"What do you mean by the Forbidden Door?" Eric asked.

"We dwarves're tunnelers. In our history we've done dug tunnels all through them mountains, don't ya know. M' ancestors dug far and deep, clear on through t' the other side o' the mountains. We only ever dug one way out o' there, though, the Forbidden Door."

"Why only one?" Kate asked.

"And why is it forbidden?" Stig asked.

"Well, the answer t' both yer questions is the same, don't ya know," Hallo replied, and his voice sank to a whisper. "The land beyond the mountains is barren an' desolate. Nothin' grows there. Everythin's dead, includin' the trees. There's a big forest beyond the mountains an' every single tree's dead. 'Bout the only things ain't dead are the Bolliwogs."

"Bolliwogs?" Eric scoffed, "What the heck's a Bolliwog?"

"I ain't never seen none, Hallo replied. "Legend says they're terrible bat-like creatures 'bout five feet long with sharp claws an' teeth, an' big leathery wings. They're covered head t' toe in fur, have big, red eyes an' a nasty attitude. They're large, fearsome brutes that'll eat yer flesh an' nibble yer bones an' pick their teeth with yer fingers."

"They sound horrible," Kate agreed.

"Sound like Muppets on steroids," Eric muttered.

"Oh, come now," said Stig, "Surely it was all just superstitious nonsense that mothers use to frighten their children when they've misbehaved."

"Well, ya may be right, birdie. I ain't sure how much truth is in them old legends," Hallo said. "But m' folk get pretty shook up anytime the Bolliwogs is mentioned. There's none gone through the Forbidden Door that's ever come back, 'cept one."

"Who was he?" Kate asked.

"Yeah, and how'd he manage to come back if these Bolliwog things are so fierce?" Eric asked.

"Well now, it were 'bout a thousand years ago, in the days o' m' granpappy."

"If I may ask, how long do dwarves live?" Stig asked.

"Well, ol' bird, I guess ya can ask 'cause ya just did, don't ya know," Hallo said. Eric thought Stig looked a little miffed. "Dwarves live 'bout five hunnert years, give or take a few decades."

"I say, not quite as long as owls but still quite impressive." Stig seemed a little smug.

"Anyways, the tunnel leadin' beyond the mountains were just finished, an' a group o' thirty dwarves were sent by the King t' explore the land beyond. They went out an' the rest o' the Kingdom waited for 'em t' come back. They were s'posed t' scout 'round for a few weeks an' then report."

"But no one ever came back, right?" Eric guessed.

"Almost, lad. A month went by an' the King were 'bout ready t' send out a search party, when ol' Creddin come back."

"Old Creddin?" Stig said. "One of the members of the exploration party, I assume."

"Ya assumes right, birdie." Hallo nodded. "I remember m' gran'pappy, who were just a little lad at the time, tellin' a bunch o' us young 'uns the tale. Creddin were mighty tore up, don't ya know. His clothes were slashed t' tatters, an' he were drippin' blood an' all. It were him what described the land beyond the mountains an' the Bolliwogs."

"So the rest of the party were all, all killed?" Kate asked. She looked a little pale. Typical girl, Eric thought.

"Aye, lass. The Bolliwogs got 'em all. Ol' Creddin managed t' get away an' back t' the tunnel. Over the next coupla centuries, a few brave, some say stupid, explorers went lookin' for adventure in the Land Beyond, but none ever come back, don't ya know. Finally, the King had a big stone door built t' block the tunnel. It were a door only he and his kin could open. For the last eight hunnert years, no dwarf has gone through the Door. In fact, it's been opened just once since."

"When Cal Endria went through, right?" Kate said.

The dwarf nodded. "Right, ya are. That were the only time. I'm shamed t' say m' folk've lived in fear since, what with Bolliwogs on one side an' Big Folk on the other."

Eric shook his head. Something didn't add up. "Cal Endria couldn't have been so stupid that he'd walk into certain death. How much did the dwarves tell him about the danger?"

"Pap used t' say that ol' Endria weren't worried none 'bout the danger," Hallo said. "From all I heard tell, he didn't believe in the Bolliwogs; thought it were wild beasts that were causin' all the trouble. Anyways, he were so keen t' get beyond the mountains, weren't no one gonna stop him, I'm a thinkin'."

"But why?" Kate asked.

"Because of another legend, lassie," Hallo lowered his voice and glanced around. The two children and the owl leaned closer, like those trying to listen in on a secret. "He found out 'bout the Jewel."

"The Jewel?" asked Eric.

"Aye, lad, the Jewel o' Paradise," Hallo's eyes were bright. "It's our oldest legend. Ya see, the legend speaks o' a jewel o' great beauty an' powerful magic in the lands beyond the Forbidden Door. It lies on the peak of a solitary mountain, guarded by a race o' wise folk. The legend goes on t' say that a hero from outside the Kingdom is the one destined t' get the Jewel, and when he does, he'll win a paradise, don't ya know.

"Pap used t' say that ol' Endria thought he'd win the Jewel sure, him bein' an outsider an' all. He figured he'd get the Jewel, explore the Land Beyond, an' lead both dwarves an' Big Folk t' a golden age."

"And the dwarves let him do it?" Kate nearly screamed.

Hallo shrugged. "More'n likely, the king wanted t' get rid o' him. Rufus Thunderhelm were like that—didn't want no outsiders knowin' 'bout the Kingdom."

"My dear dwarf, that's positively reprehensible," Stig said. Eric had to agree. It seemed a low thing to do.

"Repensiddle or no, the King didn't want no one t' go back t' yer village blabbin' that he'd been t' the Kingdom," Hallo replied. "Better t' send him on his way and not have t' deal with it anymore, don't ya know."

"So now I know what happened to Cal Endria," Kate said softly. To Eric it sounded as if she wished she didn't.

CHAPTER 8

PLANS IN MOTION

Sharky stood on the deck of his flagship, *Deathwind,* as the blood-red sun sank below the waves. His lips curled into a sneer as the wind lashed at his face and the salt spray stung his eyes. It had been a week of hard sailing by the five ships in his fleet, and still his wrath had not subsided. The ring on his finger burned with a cold fire, fanning the flames of his anger.

He watched the seagulls weave and dart among the five ships of his fleet, and his mouth formed a cruel smile. They were almost there. The gulls were a sure sign that land was near.

"Marrow!"

"Right here, Captain," Marrow said as he glided up to Sharky.

"We'll be sighting land in the morning."

"Aye, sir," Marrow hissed.

"We'll attack at dawn and crush this bloody rebellion!"

Rebellion—how dare they? The thought stoked the fire of Sharky's anger afresh. He'd been too easy on them, of course. They'd become overly comfortable in the light of his generosity. It was he who'd let Cal Endria and his lily-livered followers go off and become farmers. Endria and his cowardly folk had settled on the mainland to laze their lives away fishing and farming. The thought of such cowardice boggled his mind.

Still, Sharky thought, there was something to be said for having a base on the mainland. Perhaps, instead of cowing the swine, he should get rid of them entirely. After all, it was good land, protected from the mainland by that mountain range.

Those mountains intrigued him, too. If he could find a way over, who knew what rich plunder might be found. None of the Endrias had ever found a way—not surprising, given their lack of courage and fortitude. But it would be easy for him...

With an evil chuckle that sounded to his crew as a growl, Sharky headed aft to his cabin. Tomorrow would be a busy day.

CHAPTER 9

CALM

"Everything's falling into place," said Kate.

They were drinking lemonade around a small stone table in Kate's back garden. Light from a brass lantern in the middle of the table flickered in a summer evening breeze.

"Yeah," Eric sat back and took a sip from his glass, "everything's going pretty smoothly. The catapults and the fortifications on the ridges are done, and the net and chain will be finished in plenty of time."

"It will take a bit of doing to get both into place, I should think," Stig said.

"Ye're right about that, birdie, don't ya know," Hallo nodded. "That'll be tough work. But Cordon an' that young feller, Chip Wainscott, have a system worked out for it. Tariff Day's a month away—they'll be done on time."

Hallo had turned out to be a big help with the chain. Although a terrible blacksmith by the standards of his people, he was still better than all of Cordon's apprentices, an indication of the great craftsmanship of the dwarves. With an added pair of hands, work on the chain and spikes had been progressing ahead of schedule.

"Still, that's cutting it close," Stig frowned. "And there is still the matter of the black powder." Madame Bottleneck thought she might have the right mix—she had made up a large batch that afternoon, and was planning a final test tomorrow. "If Madame Bottleneck's formula doesn't test well, we'll be without an important weapon."

"Oh, Stig, you worry too much," Kate laughed and glanced at Eric. "Even without the black powder we've got the perfect plan. The pirates will be taken completely by surprise. Sharky will sail in, get cut off from his other ships and have no choice. He'll have to surrender."

Although he knew the preparations weren't complete, Eric was beginning to feel as confident as his friends. "It's not a perfect plan," Eric could feel himself blushing a little. "I mean, something could still go wrong."

"Nay, laddie," Hallo smiled from across the table, "it's a fine plan. They won't know which way's up, don't ya know."

"Still, I was taught not to count my chicks before they've hatched," said Stig. "We can't afford to get overly confident."

"Stig's right," the Lord Mayor walked out of the darkness into the ring of light. "We're not ready yet. If they were to come tomorrow, Sharky and his men would defeat us."

Kate turned in her chair to look at her father. "But that won't happen."

"Perhaps not." Although her father gave a hint of a smile, his eyes were sad. "But even if we're ready and the pirates are taken completely unaware, you can't expect men as bloodthirsty as Sharky to just lay down their weapons. They'll fight, and they'll fight hard, perhaps to the last man."

"You don't think they'd give up?' Eric hadn't considered that.

"It's very possible they won't," said the Lord Mayor. "I have to try to think of all possibilities. It's part of my job. Now, it's getting late. I think you should all get some sleep. We've all got work to do tomorrow."

They got up and went into the house. Eric went upstairs to the room he shared with Stig, undressed, and crawled into bed. Stig hopped up on a nightstand next to the bed. Soon, both were asleep.

Eric spent a fitful night, tossing and turning as he dreamed of the red mountain. This time, something was different. The companion in the dream wasn't his father, but Stig, Kate and Hallo. The result, however, was the same. His companions were forced off the cliff by the giant creature, which Eric now realized must be a Bolliwog.

CHAPTER 10

STORM

Eric awoke early the next morning to the sound of tapping on his window. He got up and padded across the room. In the dim predawn light, he could see a ghostly shape on the other side of the glass.

"What's that?" he asked Stig, who was perched on the sill.

"It's a seagull," the owl said. "Please open the window. I can't make out a word he's saying."

Eric opened the window. A large seagull hopped inside and began chattering in what Eric supposed to be gull talk. Stig listened calmly. When the gull had finished, Stig nodded and chirped a few times. The gull flew away.

"What's up?" Eric asked.

"Oh dear," Stig said. "It seems that the gull and his friends passed Sharky's fleet of five ships. They were headed this way."

A cold dread crept over Eric and settled like lead in his stomach. Sharky was coming. "How long until he gets here?"

"According to the gull, within the hour."

Eric nodded. This was it. Sharky was coming, and they weren't ready. Strange, he would have thought he'd be a wreck right now, but instead, he was surprised to find a sense of calm coming over himself. His stomach still felt like lead, but he knew what to do.

"Go wake Cordon and tell him to rouse the village. I'll get the Lord Mayor."

"Right," Stig said and flew out the window.

Eric pulled on his clothes as he dashed down the corridor to the Lord Mayor's room. He pounded on the door.

The Lord Mayor opened the door dressed in his nightshirt. "What is it, lad?"

Just then, there came the pealing of the meetinghouse bell.

The Lord Mayor's eyes widened. "Pirates," he gasped.

"That's right, sir," Eric said. "The gulls warned us. Sharky and five ships are about an hour away."

"Then we've still got a little time." The Lord Mayor retreated into the room and came out pulling on a pair of breeches. "Let's go."

Kate and Hallo, roused by the bell, met them in the hall. Eric filled them in as they left the house.

The Lord Mayor sent Gretchen to round up the Ladies Auxiliary to gather the children and old folk and get them to the iron mine, which was used as a makeshift shelter during emergencies.

On the Green, villagers were turning out of their homes, and farmers were coming in from the surrounding farms. It reminded Eric of what it must have been like at the start of the American Revolution in Lexington.

Everyone was gathering around the blacksmith's shop. Pushing their way through to the front of the crowd, Eric could see Stig perched on an anvil next to Cordon. The smith and his apprentices were handing out weapons.

"Ho, Charles! The scum think they'll surprise us, but we'll give them a fight!" Cordon bellowed. The eyes in the dark face blazed with battle lust. "I've waited a long time for this village to get off its backside and fight. Now Sharky and his dogs will get what's coming to them!"

The Lord Mayor grabbed a sword from Cordon and took control. Eric admired his poise. He sent Nan down to the docks with her archery group to prepare a defense. Twigg, Furrow and Mr. Flint were sent to the ridges to oversee the bombardment.

"Where's Moira?" the Lord Mayor asked.

"I'm here, Charles," Madame Bottleneck said as she fought through the throng. She was followed closely by the round form of Mrs. Casker.

"Is the black powder ready?"

"It still hasn't been tested, but I'm fairly confident. Even if we had been able to test it, I'm not sure what good it will do us."

"What do you mean?" Eric asked.

"We haven't forged any cannon, lad," Cordon said. "I've got the molds made, but we've been working on the chain. I was going to start casting cannon next week."

Eric's heart fell. What good would black powder be without cannon?

"Hey, you're the barrel lady, ain't ya?" Hallo asked, pointing to Mrs. Casker.

"That's me!" she said, giggling.

"Ya got any casks?"

"Oh land sakes, dozens! As a matter of fact, this is the time of year the farmers brew their beer. I can't make enough to please them."

"That a fact?" Hallo seemed wistful. "I'll have t' try some one o' these days, don't ya know. Anyways, we could use them casks."

"How?"

"Well, first ya drill a hole in the top an' pack 'em full of powder. Then ya stick a length of oiled rope through the hole."

"Kinda like a fuse!" Eric blurted, suddenly getting it.

" 'Xactly like a fuse. Then ya set 'em in boats, light 'em, cast 'em adrift in the harbor, an' kablooey! Could be we'll get lucky an' Sharky'll be blowed t' kingom come. Leastways, it'll cause a bunch of confusion."

Everybody grinned, and Madame Bottleneck, Mrs. Casker and Captain Weatherbee went to assemble some homemade bombs.

The crowd was thinning out as everyone went to help out with a task.

"There's nothing left to be done here," the Lord Mayor said. "We'll make a stand at the docks, Cordon."

The blacksmith nodded. "Come on then; what are we waiting for?"

"One moment," the Lord Mayor turned to Eric and the others. "You must take yourselves to the iron mine and wait there until I come and get you."

"Why do we have to go hide in the mine?" Kate's face was fierce.

"Yeah, I want to stay and fight," said Eric.

"I'm an able body," said Hallo. "I think ye're gonna need all the help ya kin git, don't ya know."

"And I could give you an aerial view of things, and perhaps marshal the seagulls," Stig said.

The Lord Mayor nodded. "Thank you. Hallo and Stig, I really could use both of you, but I have to draw the line at Eric and Kate. I can't in good conscience send children into battle."

"But, Papa, I want to fight!" Kate stamped her foot. "I'm not going to the mine, and you can't make me!"

"You can't leave us behind!" Eric was surprised at the fierce tone of his own voice. "This is as much our fight as it is yours. Stig and I've come here to help, and Kate's been practicing—she's a good shot with a bow. Hallo's right: you need all the help you can get. You need us."

"Eric, I have no hold over you, so there's nothing I can do to stop you if your mind is made up."

"It is," he said, his stomach churning.

"Very well then," the Lord Mayor nodded. "But Kate, you're my daughter, and you must obey me in this. I can't send you into danger. You're all I've got left."

"If the pirates defeat us, there won't *be* anything left!" Kate's face was livid and tears streaked down her cheeks. "I love you, Papa, and I know you're trying to protect me, but this is my village, too. I've got a right to defend it if I wish."

"Ya know, Charles," Cordon broke in, "she's right. She's got as much right as anyone to defend this bit of land. It's a hard thing, I know, but war's hard, my friend. We've all got to make sacrifices."

The Lord Mayor sighed and his shoulders sagged a bit. "I suppose you're right, Cordon. But if things go bad, we're falling back. I don't want anyone trying to be a hero. Agreed?"

Everyone nodded.

"Well then," he said, "let's go."

CHAPTER II

SURPRISE

The sun was just beginning to lighten the sky behind the mountains when Sharky's fleet reached the entrance to the harbor. In the dim light, it seemed to Sharky that all was deathly still as his flagship glided between the two ridges into the harbor.

"They're still snoozin', Mr. Marrow," Sharky rasped.

"So it seems," the first mate replied.

Suddenly, there was a whoosh and a splash. A fountain of water just off the *Deathwind's* bow cascaded over the deck.

"What in blazes?" Sharky asked, but was cut off by the sound of splintering wood behind him. Turning, he saw the main mast of the ship behind him, *Carrion,* come crashing to the deck.

"They're bombarding us with boulders, Captain," Marrow hissed.

"But how?" As Sharky watched in stunned disbelief, another boulder came tumbling out of the sky to crash through *Carrion's* deck. The ship had stopped dead in the water and was beginning to list.

Shaking his head as if coming out of a dream, Sharky roared, "Man the cannon! Them rocks're comin' from the ridges! Give 'em what for!"

Cannon fire erupted, but visibility was poor. Sharky was unable to tell if the cannon had found their mark.

"Do ye think we got 'em, Marrow?"

The answer to his question came in the form of two more boulders, one of which just missed *Deathwind*'s stern. The other ripped into *Carrion*. The beleaguered ship was taking on water. It was obvious to Sharky that she was doomed.

The pirate captain swore under his breath. Carrion was blocking the entrance to the harbor. Until she sank, he was cut off from the other three ships in his fleet.

Well, he thought, so what? *Deathwind* alone was more than a match for whatever those weak-minded villagers could think up. The other ships would take care of whatever was up on the ridges, slingshots or catapults most likely, then join him in the slaughter—for slaughter it would be.

The loss of the *Carrion* enraged him. "We take no prisoners, Marrow," Sharky growled.

"Oh goody!" Marrow said. He grinned, his emaciated face looking like death.

CHAPTER 12

BATTLE

Eric and his friends crouched behind an impromptu wall of wagons, stone and any other debris that could be found. Nan, her archers, and some other villagers were deployed along it and in the buildings nearest the harbor.

The roar of cannon erupted from across the bay. They watched as the first pirate ship entered the harbor. Sweat stood out on Eric's forehead, and his heart hammered. What were they doing? What was he doing here? They didn't stand a chance, it was obvious. Even if the catapults managed to do some damage, and if the archers were able to land some lucky arrows, they couldn't take on a fleet of five ships and expect to win—not without the chain in the harbor or the net or some cannon.

"I blew it, Stig," Eric muttered.

"What?" the owl asked.

"I screwed up. It was stupid to think that I could come up with a plan to beat Sharky."

Stig ruffled his feathers. "We're not beaten yet."

"No, but we will be soon, and it's my fault."

"You can't blame yourself my boy. They knew what they were getting into," Stig said.

"Stig's right," Kate broke in. "It's not your fault. Besides, I think we've still got a chance."

Eric shook his head and sighed. The ship was closer now. "Is that Sharky's ship?" he asked.

The Lord Mayor nodded. "That's the *Deathwind*. It's flying his flag." He pointed to a blood-red flag that fluttered from the main mast in the early morning light. The Lord Mayor frowned. "What I don't understand is what he's doing in the harbor alone. I can't make out what's happening at the entrance. Stig, could you fly up and see how things look from the air?"

"Certainly, be back in a jiffy," Stig said, and took off, flying out over the bay.

Eric watched him go, and hoped he'd be okay.

"Where are Wainscott and Weatherbee?" the Lord Mayor asked.

"They an' some fishermen got some casks of powder from ol' Bubblebeak so's they could set 'em adrift out in the harbor," Hallo said.

"For the last time, Hallo, her name is Bottleneck," Kate said.

The dwarf shrugged. "Whatever," he said.

"Where'll they be launching the boats from?" Eric asked.

"There's a little grotto over there," Kate said, pointing to where the wharf ended on their right. "It's screened off from the rest of the bay by some rocks. There's a small opening, but from the harbor it looks like a wall of stone. Captain Weatherbee keeps a sloop tied up there, and some of the fishermen dock their smaller craft and row-boats there."

Just then, there was another round of cannon fire, and Stig returned with a flutter of wings. Eric felt a surge of relief when he saw his friend return unharmed.

"What do you have to report, Stig?" the Lord Mayor asked.

"Well, it could be worse," the owl said. "It seems that the catapults did a significant amount of damage to one of the ships. It appears to be sinking. This has effectively cut off the lead ship from the others—at least until the foundering vessel sinks.

"The other three ships have picked up survivors and have begun to bombard the ridges. It doesn't look good for our friends up there, I'm afraid. They are drawing heavy fire."

Eric's mind was racing. A wild hope rose within him. "Sharky's cut off!"

"Aye, but only for a while, lad," the Lord Mayor reminded him.

"Well, let's take advantage of it while we've got the chance!" Cordon bellowed.

The Lord Mayor nodded. "Go tell Weatherbee and Wainscott to launch those boats into the bay."

Cordon grinned and rose to race off.

"No need!" cut in Stig, and pointed a wing towards the harbor.

Eric peered above the wall and saw three small boats drifting toward the pirate ship. He also saw that the ship was starting to turn. "Hey, she's coming about!"

They all watched as the ship's bow began to swing to the right so that its guns could fire a broadside at the village. No one on board the *Deathwind* seemed to have noticed the small boats in the water. The ship's bow was turning toward the floating bombs.

Eric held his breath. Would they get lucky? Suddenly, one of the boats exploded in a ball of orange and yellow flame.

Hallo shook his head. "Fuse was too short, don't ya know," he muttered.

Confused shouts and exclamations could be heard coming from the pirate ship. "They're surprised!" Eric said. "They didn't know we have black powder!"

"You're right, lad," the Lord Mayor said. "But we may have tipped our hand too soon."

Sharky's wheelman was checking the ship's turn to avoid the floating bombs, making it unable to fire a volley for the time being. However, the other two boats blew up harmlessly, enabling the *Deathwind* to come about again.

"Nan, best get your archers ready!" the Lord Mayor said.

"Right," she replied. "Everyone, light arrows!"

Fifty points of light twinkled in the dwindling darkness as the archers took aim and loosed their arrows. Many fell short, but a few found their marks, picking off gunners and starting a few small fires. As a result, only seven of the twelve cannon fired on the village.

Buildings on the hillside behind them were ripped apart. The villagers responded with more flaming arrows, trying to keep the pirates occupied in extinguishing the fires that erupted. Nevertheless, the gunners managed a second volley that raked the village once more.

Standing on the deck amid a red glow, Eric could see a large pirate waving a huge cutlass and bellowing orders.

"Is that...?" he asked.

"Yes," Kate hissed. "It's Sharky!"

"I had a feeling."

"Look, they're through!" Hallo said.

Sure enough, Eric could see three other ships coming up from behind. The ship must have sunk, Eric thought. Great, what next?

The Lord Mayor scratched his beard and bit his lip. "Hmmm. Nan, let's take some of the archers and—"

"Look!" Kate hissed, and pointed to the harbor.

A small sloop, sails billowing in the breeze, was sailing from the grotto toward the *Deathwind*. At the wheel stood the squat form of Captain Weatherbee. Chip Wainscott stood poised in the bow, a burning torch in his hand. The faces of both Council members were grim.

"What're they doing?" Eric asked.

"I don't know, lad," the Lord Mayor answered.

"They've got a bunch of powder kegs on board," Kate said. "I can see them at the bottom of the boat."

The pirates, still busy trying to extinguish the fire in the rigging, hadn't noticed the schooner's approach. It was now less than 50 yards from the ship and closing fast. When it was 25 yards away, Chip turned and lowered the torch to something in the bottom of the boat—a fuse or fuses, Eric thought.

The pirates had seen them by now. Both men hunched low as arrows came whistling down on them. Weatherbee crouched behind the wheel, but continued to steer the ship. Chip dropped the torch in the water and picked up a bow. Every so often he would stand and shoot a few arrows, before ducking a return volley. All the while the little schooner sped closer to the ship.

"Oh, jump, jump!" Kate yelled. "Why don't they jump?"

"I don't think they mean to," the Lord Mayor said through clenched teeth.

"Aye, looks like they're fixin' t' ram her, don't ya know," Hallo said.

"By jove, I do believe you're right," Stig said.

Eric didn't say anything. All he could do was stare as the little craft struck the pirate vessel amidships and exploded in a ball of flame. The blast split the pirate ship in two, throwing men and debris into the air.

CHAPTER 13

SCUTTLED

Sharky spluttered with rage and amazement as he was hauled dripping from the harbor and set down on the deck of the *Revenge,* one of the three remaining ships in his fleet. A few minutes later, Mr. Marrow was standing next to him, also dripping. They both strode to the forecastle, where Fishbane, master of the *Revenge,* awaited them.

"Stand down, Fishbane!" Sharky growled. "I'm in command o' this here vessel!"

"Aye, sir!" Fishbane said.

Sharky's knuckles turned white and his ring burned red as he clutched the rail and gazed at the village that was burning in places, but not nearly as much as he wanted it to. His face was purple with rage. Those dogs had somehow found the secret of black powder.

"Marrow!" he barked.

His first mate hovered at his side, unfazed by the chaos surrounding them. "Yes, Captain?" Mr. Marrow's voice was oily.

Blast Marrow, Sharky thought, he's cool as a corpse. Didn't anything bother that walking skeleton?

"Get the men inta the boats and lower away! It's time we gave them sheep a taste o' steel!"

"Aye, sir," said Mr. Marrow.

"Then run up the flags an' signal Bloodfoot ta bring the other ships up an' unload. I want all ships ta commence firin' on the village. We'll have them lily-livered lubbers crawlin' on their knees beggin' fer mercy!"

"Right away, Captain." The grin that broke out on Mr. Marrow's face threatened to break it in two.

He moved off down the deck, ordering men into the longboats, which were then lowered into the bay.

"No quarter," Sharky snarled to himself. "The dogs'll get no quarter from me!"

CHAPTER 14

RETREAT

E ric's face reflected the shock he saw in his companions' faces, which had gone pale.

"They didn't jump," Kate said. "Why didn't they jump?"

"I s'pose they wanted t' make sure, don't ya know," Hallo said.

"But they got Sharky, didn't they?" Eric asked, hope momentarily overcoming his shock.

"I'm afraid not," Stig said. "See, he is being hoisted aboard that ship over there. But it was a heroic act all the same."

"Stig's right. We've one less ship to deal with now," the Lord Mayor said. "Chip Wainscott and Captain Weatherbee will be hailed as heroes from this day forward."

Eric nodded as he watched the wreck of *Deathwind,* half sunk in the shallow water. Its shattered frame burned above the waterline. Barrels, planks and bodies floated in the bay. Through the smoke and flame, he could see the sails of the two remaining ships moving up to take the flagship's place.

He also saw longboats being lowered.

"Look!" he said, pointing, "They're coming ashore."

"Right," said Nan to her archers. "They're coming. Wait 'til they get ashore, then mow 'em down!"

There was a loud roar. Shells came whistling overhead and slammed into the hill behind them. The deafening explosions made their heads ring and threw clods of earth in every direction.

The Lord Mayor uttered an oath. "They're going to try to keep us pinned down here until their men get ashore."

"The other ships're unloadin', too," Hallo said.

"Hallo, Stig!" the Lord Mayor's tone was sharp.

"Yessir," Hallo said.

"At your service," said the owl.

"I want both of you to take the children out of here," the Lord Mayor ordered.

"No!" Eric and Kate yelled.

The Lord Mayor fixed them with a hard stare. "It's too dangerous here now. I cannot in good conscience continue to expose you to danger. I'm sending you to the shelter with the old folk and the other children. I want you to go there and help Gretchen and the Ladies Guild."

"I'm not going to run and hide, Papa." Kate stamped her foot. "Like I said before, Calendria is my home, too, and I'm going to fight for it!"

"I still want to stay and fight, too," Eric said. "It's what Stig and I are here for, to help you beat the pirates."

The Lord Mayor's face softened. "I'm not asking you to hide. I'm asking you for help. Gretchen will need all the help she can get to keep the little ones quiet. And if I know some of those old-timers, they'll want to come down and join the fight. They could be as much of a handful as the little ones. I need your help with this. I'll be able to concentrate better down here, knowing that you're helping Gretchen keep things in order back there.

"Besides," Eric saw the light dim in the Lord Mayor's eyes, "if things go badly here, you may be forced to fight before all is said and done."

"Oh, Papa," Kate hugged her father, her tear-streaked face pressed against his chest.

"Now, now, no tears." The Lord Mayor cupped Kate's chin in his hand, tilting her head back until their eyes met. "I need you to be brave and help Gretchen keep everyone calm. You're the Lord Mayor's daughter and your first responsibility is to your people."

Kate nodded and wiped her eyes.

"Eric," the Lord Mayor turned his gaze on the boy, "thank you for your efforts to help free Calendria."

"It wasn't anything, sir," Eric said. "I, uh, want you to know I'll do all I can to keep helping, Stig and me both will."

"Indubitably," the owl nodded his agreement.

"Er, um I hate t' break in, don't ya know," said Hallo, "but I think we'd better be gettin' while the gettin's good."

"Hallo's right," said the Lord Mayor. "Go now and good luck. If all goes well, I'll see you soon."

"C'mon, Kate," said Eric, a smile creeping onto his face. "Gretchen needs our help. She's probably pulling her hair out by now."

"If she's not," Kate said as she dried her eyes, "she will be when we get through with her. Race you!"

The two children ran off up the hill.

"Don't forget, we're in the middle of a battle!" the Lord Mayor called after them.

"Don't worry none; we'll corral 'em. Come on, owly!" Hallo stumped off after the two children, and Stig flew after him.

CHAPTER 15

A DARING PLAN

When the four arrived at the mine, they found it pretty much as the Lord Mayor had predicted. The men who were too old to fight were grumpy because they wanted to join the battle. They kept trying to leave, but their wives kept calling them back. The children, meanwhile, were wild, running around with the nervous energy that comes from being cooped up.

The mine entrance had a wrought-iron gate that under normal circumstances kept people and animals from wandering in during the night. Today, it was closed to keep people in, not out. A narrow tunnel ran 100 feet from the gate to a large chamber where mining carts and equipment were stored.

There, Gretchen and some of the other women had set up cots and blankets. A few wounded were being tended there. Overturned ore cars served as tables, and wooden buckets had been turned upside down to make chairs. Some of the old men sat around playing checkers and muttering. Children ran every which way, laughing, shouting and asking to go outside. Their mothers kept shushing them to no avail.

When Gretchen saw Eric, Stig, Kate, and Hallo, she practically ran to them. "Here you are safe and sound, thank goodness!

I've been worried sick about you all morning." Her normally perfect bun of hair was disheveled; wisps of it fell across her face. Instead of her black work dress, she wore a white blouse and a light-blue skirt. "What news from the village?"

"Well, it's not as bad as it could be," Kate said. Eric noticed that the cavern had become almost silent as everyone turned to hear the news. There were cheers when Kate told of the sinking of the two pirate ships, but they were stifled when she told of the sacrifice made by Chip Wainscott and Captain Weatherbee. The faces of her audience were troubled when she told of the impending pirate ground attack.

"On our way up here, we met Mr. Flint and Madame Bottleneck leading a large group down to the harbor. They were armed with swords and other weapons. We told them what was happening, and they rushed down the hill. A little further on, we met Mr. Twigg and Mr. Furrow and a big group of farmers with spears and pitchforks. We sent them after the others. And that's about it."

There was a great deal of grumbling from the old men as they talked among themselves. The children were much more subdued after hearing the news, and sat in small groups along the cavern walls, drawing in the dirt with sticks and talking in low voices.

Gretchen and her women went back to work, setting up a supply area and stocking it with food, clothing and medicine brought from the village. Eric and the others lent a hand until it was time for lunch.

They sat down a little way from the children and made a halfhearted attempt to eat. No one had much of an appetite. The dull rumble of cannon fire had not stopped all morning.

"Oh, I can't take this!" Kate said. "What's happening down there? I hate not knowing."

Eric nodded. "One minute, I think your father will come in and say we've won; the next minute, I'm expecting Sharky's men to turn up and clap us all in irons."

"Aye, it's worrisome, sure," Hallo said. "I guess the cannon fire's a good sign."

"How can you say that?" Kate demanded.

"Well, I mean that if the pirates're still firin', then there must still be sometin' t' fire at, don't ya know."

"Still," Eric said. "I'd like to know what's going on. Stig, could you fly down and see how the battle's going?"

"I don't see why not," the owl replied. "I'll make a quick circle around the village and fly right back."

Stig flew out of the cave. A short while later, he returned.

"The pirates have overrun the harbor. The villagers have had to fall back to the top of the hill. They've built a barricade across the ridge on the edge of the Green, but I'm afraid that the lower part of Calendria is in flames. Sharky is as mad as a hornet. He continues to bombard the village, softening it up, so to speak. He's massing his men for a frontal assault."

"We've got to do something!" Kate said.

"Aye, lass, but what?" Hallo asked. "It's just the four of us, some children an' old folk here. It's not like we got a army behind us."

Eric sat straight up. "Hallo, do you think King Rufus would help us?"

"Well now, old King Rufus has been dead an' gone for almost a hunnert years. His son, Angus, rules now." Hallo frowned. "What, you mean like send a gang o' dwarves t' fight Sharky?"

"Yeah, exactly that."

"That's brilliant!" Kate said. "We could go ask the king for help!"

"It'd be like a diplomatic mission, with Kate representing the village as the Lord Mayor's daughter!" Eric said.

"The king ain't likely t' reveal the existence o' the Kingdom just t' help a bunch o' Big Folk. 'Sides, only a dwarf can open any o' the hidden doors t' the Kingdom, an'—" the dwarf caught the knowing look on Eric's face. "Hey! I'm exiled, don't ya know. If I was t' get caught in there, I could lose m' head."

"Hallo, don't think like that," Kate said. "It's our only hope. If the dwarves don't help, Calendria is doomed."

"Yeah, and how happy do you think old King Angus would be to have a horde of pirates right outside his precious Kingdom?" Eric asked. "Seems to me that'd be a lot more alarming than what he's got now."

"Yeah, but I can't, oh well o' course I can't let that happen…not after all you folk've done for me, don't ya know," Hallo spluttered. "I'll get ya inta the Kingdom, but we'll need a whole passel o' luck t' get any farther."

"Then it's settled; we leave as soon as we can slip away," Eric said. The others nodded.

CHAPTER 16

MISSION

It wasn't until late afternoon that the two children and the dwarf went up the tunnel with the owl flying alongside. At the entrance, they eased open the gate, trying to avoid making any noise that would alert anyone back inside. Once out, they headed toward the monument, then up the path into the mountains. The daylight was almost gone and a full moon was rising when they arrived at the dead end. The sheer cliff gleamed white in the twilight.

Eric passed his hand over the wall's smooth stone face. "It sure looks solid, Hallo. If you hadn't said there was a door here, I never would have known."

"Aye, that's the way o' dwarf doors, laddie," said Hallo. "As I said before, only a dwarf can open 'em, don't ya know."

Hallo placed his left hand, palm outward, against the rock. For a moment, nothing happened. Then Eric thought it seemed to quiver. Gradually, the outline of a large doorway appeared. The outline solidified, and the door swung inward slowly, revealing a dark passageway.

Eric peered inside, a cold shiver running through him. "It's darker than I thought it'd be."

"Don't ya worry none 'bout that, lad. All we have t' do is step inside," said Hallo. "C'mon, let's go."

They all stepped through the door. A soft light began to glow from above, revealing an arched hallway chiseled out of the stone. The floors were smooth, and detailed images of dwarves, some fierce, some kind, were carved into the walls. Eric had never seen anything like it. They gave him chills.

"Them carvin's trace the hist'ry o' the dwarves from the beginnin' right up t' today, don't ya know," said Hallo. "The walls o' every passageway're carved like this. There's many inlaid with silver an' gold or precious gems further in, you'll see."

"I say," Stig exclaimed, "it's all rather impressive. These reliefs are exquisite."

"If the dwarf kingdom is all like this, Hallo," said Kate, "then it's a hidden jewel."

"Where's the light coming from?" asked Eric.

"It's a moss what gives off light when the warmth from a person is near. We call it glowmoss. This is the side door, an' this passage ain't used much, so it's mostly dark. The more traveled ways're lit 'most all the time. We'll have t' go on a little ways t' get t' the inhabited parts."

The passage was straight and descended gradually. The carvings on the walls became even more detailed as they went on. Soon they came to a smaller passage to the left of the one they followed. Hallo, who had taken the lead, called a halt.

"Here's as far as we go t'day, don't ya know," he said. "We'll bed down in here."

He led them into the side passage, which turned out to be a small room hewn out of the rock. There was a cooking pit in the center of the floor that contained glowing rocks topped by an iron cooking grate. In a corner of the room were two large jugs. Eric checked them out and found water in one and ale in the other. Next to the jugs were a small table and four chairs. A sleeping alcove was cut into each of the three walls, so the dwarf and the children each took one and stowed their gear. Stig perched on a shelf in Eric's alcove. When they'd settled in, they fixed dinner, heated on the glowing stones, and sat down to eat.

"Hallo, what is this place?" asked Eric. "And how do these stones stay so hot?"

"This is a way station, fer travelers in the dwarf kingdom," said Hallo as they ate. "They come in mighty handy, don't ya know. As for the stones, they're called hotstones. We find 'em when we're minin'. Come in mighty useful. We use 'em t' cook and fer heatin' our forges. Better'n fire. There's no smoke t' vent, and they don't ever burn out."

"What happens now, Hallo? How long until we get to the king?" Kate asked, stifling a yawn.

"The king lives in Stonedeep, a large city in the center o' the Kingdom. It's a good day's march or more. Since we're comin' at Stonedeep from the side, we ain't gonna get there as quick as if we took the main door, but we'll see fewer folk, which is what we want."

"What would happen if we were to run into anyone, Hallo?" Stig asked.

"Well now, I ain't sure," Hallo squinted at the owl across the cooking pit. "I'm in exile, don't ya know, an' they won't be none too pleased t' see me, I'm a-thinkin'. Then agin, I'm not what you'd call a threat or dangerous or anythin', so we may be able t' get through okay. It'll be tough gettin' inta Stonedeep, though. I'm a thinkin' we'll see King Angus, but prob'ly as prisoners. Still, if we can just see his majesty, we'll have a chance t' convince him t' help Calendria, and that's all that counts, ain't it?"

Eric nodded without saying anything. When they'd finished eating, they all turned in for the night. Eric was having a hard time adjusting to the perpetual light of the dwarf kingdom. It gave him a feeling of timelessness that was unnerving. It took him a long time to fall asleep. From across the room, he could hear the loud snores of the dwarf.

"Stig," he whispered.

Above him, the owl shifted on the shelf. "Yes?"

"I can't sleep."

"I must confess that I'm having a hard time myself," said the owl.

"Are we doing the right thing?" Eric asked.

"How do you mean?"

"Well, I don't like all this talk of being taken prisoner. Maybe we should have stayed to fight."

"In these situations, Eric, I've found that one should follow one's instinct. That's why we're here. In this case, I think that Hallo is right. The point is to see the king. That's the most important thing; how we do that doesn't really matter."

"I guess so," Eric sighed. "It felt like the right thing to do in the mine. It's just that now that we're here, I'm not sure anymore."

"I think you'll feel much better after a good night's rest. Things will look better in the morning, you'll see. Now let's get to sleep, we've another long day ahead of us."

"Okay. Thanks, Stig. Sleep well."

"Goodnight, Eric," said Stig.

CHAPTER 17

PRISONERS

Eric was awakened by a pain in his chest. When he opened his eyes, he found himself looking at the sharp point of a spearhead inches away from his face. It was held by a black bearded dwarf in full battle armor.

"Get up young'n," the dwarf's voice was harsh, "nice and slow-like."

Eric eased himself up out of his bedding. The dwarf indicated the main room with his spear.

"Get over there by the cookpit with the rest o' your gang. Hey, hang on, this your bird?"

Eric looked up at Stig, who still perched on the shelf. "Uh, yeah, he's mine."

"Well take 'im with ya. I don't want 'im flyin' 'round loose. He got a leash?"

"Uh, no."

"Well, here," the dwarf tossed Eric a leather thong. "Tie that 'round his leg."

"Come here, Stig," said Eric. Stig flew to the ground beside him.

"Oh, ya got him trained, eh?"

"Yeah, he does all sorts of tricks," Eric said.

"Well, tie him up, all the same. I ain't gonna be pecked t' death by no bird."

Eric tied the leather leash to Stig's leg, and the two joined Hallo and Kate at the cooking pit. There were three other dwarves, each clad in blue armor and armed like the one who had woken Eric. Kate was very red in the face as she stood fuming between two dwarves, but Eric thought she looked scared, too. Hallo was trying to reason with a dwarf with a yellow braided beard who seemed to be in charge.

"Now, Cap'n," said Hallo, "why might ya be disturbin' travelers from their sleep? Have we been doin' anythin' wrong?"

"We got a report last night that the side door had been opened. We were sent t' investigate. Now here you are, a dwarf with two Big Folk cubs and some sort o' bird. An' I'm wantin' an explanation. Where're ya headed? Why'd ya let them in, 'cause I know they couldn't get in themselfs, an' who are *you*?"

Hallo licked his lips and fiddled with his orange beard. "Well, sir, the name's Hallo, Hallo Tosis. I'm from the village o' East Cavern, originally, but I bin away fer a spell, don't ya know. These here children're folk as I met on m' wanderin's, an' I was givin' 'em kind of a tour, don't ya know."

The captain squinted in disbelief. "Hallo Tosis, what type o' name is that fer a dwarf? It cain't be yer real 'un. 'Sides, ya should know strangers ain't allowed t' be brung in."

"Hey, I know him, Cap'n," said the dwarf guarding Eric. "He's that dwarf what was exiled a ways back. Couldn't do nuthin' dwarfish, a real disgrace!"

"Is that true?" the captain's eyes had a steely glint.

Kate shot a quick glance at Eric, who looked at Hallo. The poor dwarf was sweating buckets.

"Well, um, nnn, uh," Hallo stuttered. "Ya might say that. It were all a misunderstandin' 'tween me an' m' pappy. Ya see—"

"Hey now, that's enough o' that," the captain interrupted, "Yer all under arrest fer enterin' the Kingdom unlawfully. We be takin' ya t' Rockhaven, the nearest village. The authorities there'll decide what's t' be done with ya."

The dwarves bound the hands of the prisoners and gathered up the travelers' belongings. They were led out of the roadhouse, and the party headed toward Rockhaven.

Their captors set a fast pace. Hallo, with his sturdy dwarf legs, had no problem, but the others were hard pressed. One of the dwarves was forced to carry Stig, whose leash was too short to allow him to fly. They continued on in this way for the rest of the morning before stopping all too briefly to eat something from their packs. Within a half-hour they resumed their excruciating pace.

Shortly after lunch, the passage merged with one that opened on their right, in much the same way, Eric noted, as the entrance ramp onto a highway. They now began to meet a number of travelers—dwarves carrying packs or pulling wagons—headed either in their direction or back toward the adjoining passage.

The traffic became thicker as they marched on, forcing their captors to slow the pace. It seemed to Eric, though, that they were still going very quickly. His legs were beginning to cramp when they arrived at a large archway. Two stone outposts sat on either side of the opening. They were manned by a number of armored dwarves. A black-bearded dwarf strode over to meet them as they came to a halt. He carried a long spear under his arm.

"G'day, Cap'n," he gave a casual salute. "Whatcha got?"

"I got me these here prisoners, sergeant. Caught 'em usin' one o' the hospitality holes. Gonna throw 'em inta the lockin 'til we get word what t' do with 'em," the captain replied with a grin.

"What's that?" the sergeant pointed to Stig with his spear.

"A pet o' the boy's," said the dwarf holding Stig. He held the owl out for the sergeant to see, and nodded at Eric. "He's got 'im trained, comes when he calls an' everythin.'"

"All right, all right," said the captain. "That's enough jawin'. We gotta get a move on."

"Ye're clear t' pass," said the sergeant. "I'll be seein' ya lads at the pub after duty, I s'pose."

"Aye, see ya, Sarge," the captain grinned and slapped him on the back.

The prisoners were marched under the arch and into Rockhaven, a village built into the walls of a large cavern. The ceiling was illuminated, presumably by glowmoss, but it was much brighter than the passage. There was another arch in the wall on the far end of the cavern. The walls to the left and right of them were dotted by row upon row of what looked to be doorways. A high stone stairway rose on either end of each wall. Dwarves scurried like ants along the ledges that ran along the front of each level.

Eric gasped when he saw the walls of dwellings, which rose like two tall apartment buildings. The sheer height was not what took his breath away, though. The entire wall was covered with a green, ivy-like plant growing up from the base of each wall. Dotted here and there, like a million points of color, he could see flowers of yellow, red, purple, orange, blue—every color of the rainbow. It gave such a profound feeling of life to that land of stone, that his eyes were filled with it. He saw that dwarves tended the plant in the area around their dwelling, as if it were a garden, and realized that, for them, it was.

Eric tore his gaze from the walls as they were hustled into the village. The dwarves conducted their commerce on the floor of the cavern. Shops were set up in blocks with open areas—roads he realized—that were arranged in an orderly grid. Sights and smells, some familiar and some strange, came rushing at him as they were marched toward the far end of the cavern. He heard the buzz of conversation and the shouts of merchants hawking their wares, reminding him of a Middle Eastern bazaar he'd seen in a movie.

They marched through the entire length of the market, emerging in front of the arch at the other side. The captain led them toward the stairs on the left. When they reached the foot of the stairs, he halted and turned to address them.

"Now then. We'll be goin' up in a minute," he pointed toward the uppermost row. "All the way up." Eric felt queasy.

"Now some o' ya might be a little squeamish 'bout the height. Don't worry, ye'll be just fine with us. We'll go as slowly as ya like for this part o' the journey, but it's better goin' up faster than slower if ya don't like heights. Let's go."

The group began their long climb to the top. The stairs were about six feet wide and set into the corner of the chamber so that by keeping close to the wall on their right, and looking up instead of down, Eric found it wasn't that bad. The climb was long, though. Every ten feet they climbed there was a ledge that served as a walkway to the homes on that level. Each ledge was carved from the living rock of the wall and was very thick at the base before tapering off to a few feet thick at the edge. Eric had counted twenty levels when they arrived at the top.

The ceiling was much closer now, so that when Eric looked up, he was dazzled by the light. At this range, he was able to see that golden stars dotted the ceiling. They were about 4 feet wide from point to point and made of solid gold. The stars were, in fact, reflecting the light from the moss, which grew in the center of each star.

"Living light bulbs," he muttered to himself as he gazed in wonder.

The captain marched them down the row of dark openings. Eric saw that the ledge was nice and wide—about 10 feet or so. The captives were led to a doorway in the wall at the center of the level. An iron gate was built into the opening. Here they halted. The captain pulled a large silver key out of his pocket and inserted it into the gate, which swung silently outward on well-oiled hinges.

"All right, you lot," he gestured toward the door with his spear, "inside now, quick."

The prisoners were herded into the cell, and the captain shut the door with a clang.

"We need t' see the King," Hallo gripped the bars of the gate and glared out at the captain. "I invoke the Rights o' Dwarfdom t' speak with the King!"

"Listen you, exiled dwarfs don't have no rights," the captain sneered. "Ya don't exist."

Kate came forward to stand behind Hallo. She looked the captain in the eyes, but when she spoke, her tone was a little breathless.

"My name is Kate Endria, and my father, Charles Endria, is Lord Mayor of Calendria. I'm an ambassador for my village. I really need to speak with the King. Our village is under attack from a fierce band of pirates. My people need your help. Hallo offered to guide us, even though he knew he'd get in trouble if he came back. It's very important; the survival of Calendria could depend on it."

"Well now," the captain frowned, "that's a diff'rent story. I s'pose I could send a message along and then we'll see. The king's ministers'll decide what's t' be done. I'm afraid that's all I can do, lass."

"Thank you, captain," Kate replied, "I appreciate it."

The captain saluted and left, followed by the guards. The prisoners turned and examined their quarters.

Their cell was actually quite spacious. It was lit by glowmoss that grew on the walls where they met the ceiling. Four bunks of stone were carved into the walls, each made up with a mattress and bedclothes. A stone table and four chairs were in the center of the room. The children, exhausted from their forced march, slumped into them. Hallo sat down as well, while Stig perched on the table.

"Now what?" asked Eric.

"Well, I suppose all we can do now is wait," said Stig.

"I guess, but for how long?" asked Kate.

"We could be waitin' a long time, lassie," Hallo sighed. "An outcast dwarf an' a young girl ain't the most compellin' reasons t' respond, don't ya know."

"But Calendria's in trouble," said Kate. "Doesn't that count for anything?"

"I wouldn't pin m' hopes on it," Hallo shook his head. "The king might agree t' see us, or he might just let us sit here 'til we're old an' gray."

"There's got to be something we can do," Eric said.

"Fer now, we'll just have ta sit tight, don't ya know," Hallo shrugged. "It's all we kin do."

CHAPTER 18

HOLDING ON

It was the second day of the battle. Although the pirates had taken the harbor, the villagers were not dismayed. They still held the hill leading up to the center of the village, and fought with determination. By doing so, they'd learned they could stand toe to toe with their brutal foe.

The Lord Mayor stood at the top of the hill under the shelter of a large oak. He stared unseeing out over the harbor in the early morning light. His trembling hand clutched a letter. He didn't hear Madame Bottleneck as she approached, hardly noticed as she placed a hand on his shoulder.

"What's the matter, Charles?" she asked.

"Hmm? Oh, hello, Moira." The Lord Mayor turned and gave his friend a weary smile. "You mean what's wrong besides all that?" He waved a hand toward the harbor.

"Besides all that." She gave a small smile.

"Oh, Kate's run off with Eric, Hallo and Stig."

"Run off?" Madame Bottleneck raised her eyebrows. "Where to, for heaven's sake?"

The Lord Mayor handed her the letter. The apothecary read it, her smile growing as she did.

"That's some daughter you've got, Charles."

The Lord Mayor nodded. "I know. She's got spirit, that's for sure."

"You never know; she just might come back with help."

The Lord Mayor turned and looked at her. "A girl, a boy, a bird and an outcast dwarf? I'd say the odds are long, Moira."

"Still, long odds haven't stopped her before. She was the only one who went looking for the Deliverers, and she found them."

Charles nodded and looked out into the haze that hung over the harbor. "Kate's so much like her mother. I don't want to lose her, too."

"Olivia never stopped fighting, not even when the fever wracked her body. She kept experimenting, trying to find a cure, not just for herself, but for everyone afflicted with the fever. She did it, too, but not until it was too late to save herself. She was my best assistant and my best friend. She would have made a fine apothecary after me, but she wasn't able to save herself, and I wasn't either..." Madame Bottleneck's voice trailed off, and her face had a sad, wistful look.

Charles stood by her and held her hand in both of his. "You did your best. By the time a cure was found, there wasn't anything anyone could do. But that's why I worry about Kate. What if she shares her mother's fate?"

"That's out of your hands, dear," Moira said. "But if you ask me, I think she'll return to you. She's on a mission to help save her village, and that will drive her, just as it will drive us to defeat those who oppress us."

"Do you think so, Moira?" the Lord Mayor looked down at her.

Madame Bottleneck's clear blue eyes sparkled behind her glasses. "Charles, I'm sure of it."

CHAPTER 19

JEREMIAH TOSIS

When the guard brought them breakfast, they asked him if there was any news, but he just shook his head. Kate was especially frantic.

"Why don't we hear something?" she asked.

"Kate, that's got to be the hundredth time you've asked that," Eric almost shouted.

"So? We've got to hear something soon or Calendria's going to be wiped out," she said, fighting back tears. "For all we know, Sharky and his men have killed everyone and burned the town to the ground."

"Hopefully, that is not the case," said Stig, "but what more can we do? We can only sit here until the king decides to answer our message."

"Yeah, but he ain't known t' be quick about these things," Hallo shook his head.

"That's not good enough!" Kate stamped her foot. "Can't we have the captain send a message to someone else?"

"Like who?" asked Eric.

"I don't know—a lawyer, or a government official, someone the king will listen to. Hallo, don't you know anyone?"

"Well, there's lots o' people I know, but none what could help us," said Hallo. " 'Cept, maybe, Pap. He's the royal goldsmithy, a right important position. But I can't see him liftin' so much as a finger t' help me."

"Still, it's our only shot," said Eric.

"It's better than nothing," said Kate. "At least if we send a message to your father, I'd feel like we're doing everything we can."

"I s'pose you're right," Hallo sighed. "But I ain't gettin' m' hopes up. Pap washed his hands o' me when he disowned me. He ain't likely to change his mind none."

"Where does he live, Hallo?" Eric asked.

Hallo tugged at his beard. "A village called Silverlode. It's the gateway t' Stonedeep, which is the center o' the Kingdom an' the center o' government."

"We should call the captain and see if he could get Hallo's father a message," Eric said.

As it turned out, there was no need. Just before lunch, the captain came with news. "We're a-goin' on a journey," he said.

"Where are you taking us?" Eric asked.

"Seems that ya got important friends. The Royal Goldsmithy says he'll get ya in t' see His Majesty."

"I cain't believe it." Hallo scratched his beard. "It ain't like m' pappy t' do no favors fer me, don't ya know."

"It ain't on account o' you," the captain snapped. "The message we got was addressed t' the lass." He pulled a rumpled piece of parchment from his pocket and handed it to Kate.

"To Kate Endria, descendent of Calvin Endria, greetings," Kate read aloud. "Word has reached me of your plight and the attack upon your village. I understand that you and your companions have come on a diplomatic mission to ask our esteemed King Angus Thunderhelm for his help to drive the devils from your land.

"As someone of no small importance to His Majesty, I have taken it upon myself to ask him to grant you an audience. He, in his wisdom, has given his consent, and I have been instructed to present you to him myself as soon as possible. Therefore, you are to be escorted to me at Silverlode immediately. From there, I shall accompany you to Stonedeep, the royal centerpiece of the Kingdom. I look forward to meeting both yourself and your companion shortly. With kindest regards, Jeremiah Tosis, Royal Goldsmithy."

"Companion?" Eric asked. "What did he mean by that? You've got more than one companion, Kate."

"He's referrin' t' you, Eric." Hallo sighed. "Stig's just a bird t' him, an' I don't count. I'm exiled, don't ya know."

"But why would your father be so interested in me?" Kate asked.

"I ain't got no idea," Hallo said, shrugging.

"You folk eat lunch quick," the captain said. "Then we'd best be gettin' on our way."

They decided to eat as they walked. Kate was eager to get going, and the rest agreed. Everyone was driven by the thought that any delay could be disastrous.

The captain and two of his men escorted them. Once again, Eric kept to the wall as he descended the stairs. As they walked, Hallo told them about Stonedeep.

"Silverlode's a purty city, but Stonedeep—there ain't nothin' t' compare."

"How far of a march is it from Silverlode to Stonedeep?" Kate asked.

"From Pap's house, it's an hour through the city an' yer there."

Kate frowned.

"Ya see," Hallo explained, "Stonedeep's really a big palace, well, a huge palace. Big as a city it is, but no one don't live there. Everyone workin' in the government, 'cept the king and his family, lives in Silverlode."

They marched hard for the rest of the day, and spent the night in a hospitality hole. The next morning, they resumed their journey at the same quick pace. Eric's feet were aching when they finally came to the gates of Silverlode just before noon.

The huge gates were flung wide and a guardhouse was dug into the left-hand side of the corridor. Eric counted fifty guards. Some stood at attention in a line along each door of the gate, the light glinting on their spears and their reddish mail shirts. Others checked travelers entering and leaving the city.

"They've got a lot of security," Eric said.

"Sure they does, it's the heart o' the Kingdom," the Captain pointed at the guards. "Them's the Imperial Guard. They's the only ones can wear the Red Mail. See that one with the silver braid in his beard? That's the Imperial Captain. Technically, we're both the same rank, but, really, we ain't. He outranks me, 'cause he's got the Red Mail." The captain sighed. "Mebbe one day, I'll get the duty. 'Course I'd have t' start as a private, but it's important duty."

The Captain and his men brought the group up to the Imperial Captain and gave him a salute. He returned the salute, giving the Captain what seemed to Eric to be a haughty look.

"State yer name, base and business, Captain," he demanded.

The captain drew himself up. "Cap'n Ezekiel Dimbledoll, from out Rockhaven ways, yer Lordship. We're takin' these here folk t' the Royal Goldsmithy at his request."

The Imperial Captain raised an eyebrow. "From one o' the outer villages, eh? Capt'n, I want you an' yer men t' oil yer mail t'night. Yer lookin' a wee bit shabby."

Captain Dimbledoll went red with embarrassment. "Aye, sir, that we will."

"Good." The Imperial Captain nodded. "Yer clear t' proceed."

"Thank'ee, yer Lordship." Dimbledoll saluted and led them through the large arched gate into the city.

Eric was amazed at its size. The walls to the left and right of the entrance were filled with homes that were covered with the stunning vines and flowers, just as he'd seen in Rockhaven. The walls went up much higher, however—probably thirty-five or forty stories. The marketplace was very different. Magnificent golden statues of dwarves—all very detailed and lifelike—lined the central avenue. Eric thought that they must be of past heroes and kings. Each stood on a 10-foot-tall pedestal encrusted with gems of every description; clear diamonds, green emeralds, red rubies, blue sapphires and multicolored opals.

The boy's eyes widened as he took in the beautiful spectacle. He was tempted to walk over to one of the statues for a closer look, but decided now was not the time for sightseeing. Captain Dimbledoll marched them down a street, which led straight back to the high wall of dwellings. As he looked up, he breathed a sigh of relief. Hallo had told him that his father's house was in the center of the bottom level. The dwarf had said with a small hint of pride that it was a mark of honor that the house was placed so.

The Captain led them to an ornately sculpted gold door. As they stood on the marble front steps, Eric could tell right away that whoever had wrought it was a master of his craft. The door told the tale of the Tosis family's history from its beginning up to the present day. Finely detailed dwarves—all Tosis ancestors—seemed to rise out of the door itself. Each was shown doing what he was best known for.

Some were depicted performing great acts of courage; a few, sculpting some of the fine stone reliefs that ran throughout the Kingdom. Most were of dwarves doing wondrous things with gold.

The last dwarf shown was one of these. He held a finely wrought crown, the most beautiful thing anyone in the family had ever made, but on his face was a scowl that made Eric cringe. It was a look of anger and disappointment, but also pain. He knew it was the face of Jeremiah Tosis. The space on the door beside Jeremiah was blank.

Hallo followed Eric's gaze. "That should be m' own space," the dwarf said quietly. "But I'm exiled, don't ya know, so it'll be forever blank."

Eric felt a pang of sorrow for his friend.

The Captain pulled a red silken cord that hung to the left of the door. From inside, they heard the tinkling of little bells, then heavy footsteps pounding the floor to the door, which was jerked open.

A dwarf stood in the doorway peering at them. Eric recognized Jeremiah Tosis from his likeness on the door. The dwarf was wearing brown breeches and black boots, a white linen shirt and a leather vest. His long red beard was streaked with gray.

"Ah, yer here," he grunted. His green eyes looked at each of them, but passed over Hallo. "Come in, come in. Thank'ee, Cap'n, for bringin' 'em over. Watch that other one, will ya?" He jabbed a thumb in Hallo's direction.

"Aye, yer Lordship, that we will," said the Captain. He and his men surrounded Hallo and led him off toward the marketplace.

"Where are they taking Hallo?" Kate demanded.

"He's an exile," Jeremiah snapped. "They're lockin' him up."

"You can't do that," she said. "He's part of our mission."

"Yer speakin' o' somethin' ya don't know." Jeremiah's eyes were hard. "An exile don't have no rights. He'll stay locked up 'til we see the King.

"Now come along in." He stood aside and beckoned them in. "We've got lots t' talk about."

Eric and Kate went in, and Stig flew after them. Although made of stone, the dwelling was comfortable. Satin cushions lined the two stone couches that faced a pit in the corner of the great room, where hotstones gave off a warm glow. Directly across from the door, another doorway led to the rest of the house. A large stone table and chairs sat in the center of the room. A great woven rug covered the floor, and small tapestries hung on all four walls. These were woven in red, blue, green and gold. Eric thought the gold could be actual golden thread.

Stig perched on the table and the two children sat down while Jeremiah stood before them. "All right, what's this all about? Ya say Calendria's in trouble?"

The children nodded. "Yes, sir," said Kate, "the pirates have attacked it. My father, the Council and the other villagers are trying to fight them off."

"When did all this start?" Jeremiah asked.

"Four days ago," she said.

"What made ya think the dwarves'd help?"

"Your son thought if we could get a message to King Angus, he might help," Eric said.

"So ya all went with him inta the Kingdom." Jeremiah made a face. "I s'pose he didn't tell ya what t' expect? He's an outcast an' shoulda known better'un t' bring Big Folk inta the Kingdom."

"He knew that," Eric shot back, annoyed. "He's trying to help Calendria."

"Well, and you were caught. Good thing Cap'n Dimbledoll thought t' get ahold'a me."

"That's just what we had decided," Eric said. "We were going to ask the Captain to get a message to you. Hallo said you'd be the only one who could help. He thought you wouldn't help, because of him, but he's your son, so—"

"Son? Son!" Jeremiah's anger was sudden and fierce. "Why d' ya keep yammerin' on about m' son?! I have no son! I did oncet, but no more. Do ya know what a disgrace that lad is? 'Cuz o' him I can't hold m' head up in public no more. Me, the finest goldsmithy in the Kingdom!

"I'm not unreasonable, ya understand. I realize not everyone's cut out t' be a goldsmithy. That's fine. Some members o' the family've been fine stone masons, silversmithys, sculptors. One was even a blacksmithy! But the lad can do none o' them things! He ain't cut out for nothin'. Now tell me what I'm s'posed t' do with someone like that?"

Stig shook his head. "He thought you'd be like this."

"Wonderful!" Jeremiah threw his hands in the air. "Maybe he shoulda been a soothsayer! I mean, what's he want me t' do? I disowned him, I can't reown him!"

Suddenly, the old dwarf realized who had spoken. His eyes widened as he looked at Stig, and his lips moved wordlessly.

"He knows that!" Eric's anger welled up, and he took advantage of Jeremiah's shock to let him know what he thought of the whole situation. "He's not asking you to 'reown him.' He's not asking for anything for himself. He wants you to help us complete our mission. That's the only reason he agreed to come."

Jeremiah was still staring in amazement at Stig. "Ya can talk?"

"Quite so," Stig said calmly. "I have been able to do so all of my life."

"Well, I'll be hornswoggled." Jeremiah stroked his beard in thought, then turned his gaze from the owl to the children.

"His motives may be good," he said of Hallo, "but that still ain't no excuse for comin' back with all o' ya."

The old dwarf sighed, and his eyes stared into space. The hotstones gave off a red glow, making the left side of the dwarf's face look flushed while the right side was black with shadow. It seemed to Eric that they sat in silence forever.

Finally, Jeremiah sighed again and sank down into a seat. He stared into the pit of hotstones.

"I doubt the King'll give his okay," he murmured.

"Why not?" Eric asked.

Jeremiah turned his gaze back to them. " 'Cause it ain't never been done before."

"But nevertheless, we've got to try," Stig said. "We've got no other hope."

Jeremiah nodded and spoke to Kate. "I'll see what I can do, lassie."

"Thank you, Jeremiah," Kate said. Eric saw the grateful look through the tears that stood in her eyes. "We appreciate anything you can do."

"I'm just wondering why," Eric said, still seething over the dwarf's callous disregard for his son. "If you're telling the truth and it's not because of Hallo, then why do you want to help us?"

"I got m' reasons." Jeremiah's voice was gruff. "I'll send a message t' His Majesty t'night askin' for an audience tomorrow. It's gettin' late. Let's eat and get t' bed. Tomorrow's gonna be busy."

CHAPTER 20

A WINDOW ON THE PAST

The next morning, Jeremiah led them out of the house. Waiting outside was Hallo surrounded by Captain Dimbledoll and his two guards. Hallo's face was pale and drawn.

"Captain," Jeremiah said, "I'll take charge o' the prisoner."

"Aye, m'lord," the Captain gave a half salute and turned to Kate and Eric. "Well, lass and laddie, it's been fine knowin' ya. Good luck with yer mission, and take care o' yerselfs."

"Thank you, Captain." Eric shook the dwarf's hand. "And good luck to you, too. Maybe you'll get to wear the Red Mail one day."

"Aye, laddie." The Captain gave a wistful smile. "Maybe I will one day at that."

"Goodbye, Captain. Thank you for your help. Without you, we'd still be in jail." Kate flung her arms around his neck and kissed his cheek.

Dimbledoll blushed. " 'Tweren't nothin', lass. Anyone woulda' done it."

"I can't tell you how grateful we all are to you, my good Captain," Stig said.

Dimbledoll gaped at Stig, eyes wide. "Er, um, mmm, huh?" was all he could manage as they bade him goodbye.

Jeremiah led them down the street toward the main avenue. When they reached it, he led them left. Ahead, though still a good way away, they could see the large arch that led to Stonedeep. The street was busy with pedestrians and carts that were pulled or pushed by their owners. Everyone they passed turned their heads and stared at the humans as they passed by.

Eric and Kate walked on either side of Jeremiah and asked him questions about the Kingdom, while Hallo walked a couple of paces behind and Stig flew beside him.

"When did the dwarves first come here?" Eric asked.

"The Kingdom is more'n three thousand years old. It were founded by Orvis the Red, who come from over the sea. He thought the mountains'd be rich in gold an' gems, an' he were right, by gum. They was a ton! He become King Orvis I, an' it were he what ordered the first carvin's in the High Road t' commemorate the journey. At first, Silverlode an' Stonedeep were the only towns. The High Road were the only passage, an' there were only one entrance, what's now called Center Gate. As time went on, the ancestors carved out more an' more passages an' discovered an' enlarged the caverns that become Rockhaven an' the rest."

"What about the Forbidden Door?" It was a question that had been burning inside Eric since Hallo had first told them of it.

"Aye, well, seein' as how someone's already told ya summat about it," Jeremiah shot a glance over his shoulder at Hallo, "I don't s'pose it'll hurt t' tell ya. It's our darkest secret an' our deepest shame.

"We dug clear through the mountains, ya see. On the other side there's a land as bleak an' terrible as yer side be green and purty. The fur side was home t' some creatures as shouldn't o' been disturbed. It ain't written what they was, but they was dark and terrible, so the tales say. Anyways, the short end o' the story is that a door were placed at the end o' the passage leadin' t' that land—a dwarf door just like the one ya used t' enter the Kingdom. Only thing is, it cain't be opened by anybody. The only thing that'll open it is a special key that the King has. He's the only one what can open the Forbidden Door."

"Is that how Cal Endria got in?" asked Kate, wide-eyed.

"Aye, lass." The old dwarf looked at her, and the hard glint in his eyes softened slightly. "King Rufus Thunderhelm granted him leave t' pass through the Door, the only time such a thing's happened. I was there t' see it happen. Ya see lass, Cal Endria were m' friend. I wanted t' go with him, but the king wouldn't allow it."

"Huh?" Hallo stopped short, a look of astonishment on his face. "Well, I'll be. You ain't never mentioned this before, Pap."

"An' why should I!" the old dwarf snapped, turning on his son. "I don't have t' go explainin' m'self t' the likes o' you. 'Sides, it weren't nothin' but young foolishness. I was naught but a lad when it happened."

"Were you and Cal Endria good friends, Jeremiah?" Kate asked.

"If it weren't for your ancestor, I wouldn't be a standin' here today," Jeremiah said.

"How did you meet? What was he like?" Kate asked. "There's so much I want to know about him."

"Well, lass," the old dwarf said, "he were a great man, as ya must've heard. He were different from other Big Folk that m' folk've chanced on, present company excepted. We was both 'bout 60, young for a dwarf. In fact, I were a lad just apprenticed. Mind ya, it were over three hundred years ago.

"Things were different then. The Kingdom were in an uproar 'bout the new human settlement by the bay. When they first come, we watched 'em t' see what they'd do, whether they'd stay or not. After a few years when it looked like they was not only stayin' but growin', King Rufus an' his ministers got real jumpy. They figured that the men'd start lookin' fer a way over or under the mountains sooner or later, an' they didn't want t' be discovered an' p'raps forced out o' the Kingdom.

"M' pappy worked as chief goldsmithy in Stonedeep. He were always bringin' home news from the palace, were m' pappy, so when he would talk o' the men by the bay, I got the notion t' see 'em fer m'self.

"Late one night, I slipped out o' the house an' made m' way t' the Side Gate. When I got there, there weren't nobody in sight, so I just walked on through.

"When I got out, I wandered 'round a bit, tryin' t' get m' bearin's. I'd been out a few times before, but never by m'self. By mornin', I were good an' lost. Them mountain passes all looked the same t' me, an' what looked like paths broke off inta nothin'.

"M' pappy said later he had dwarves out lookin' for me, but they had t' be careful so's not t' be seen. I must've been wanderin' for more'n two weeks without a thing t' eat. Finally, I lay m'self down on a rock ledge, close t' done in from starvin'.

"Then, real sudden-like, there was a shadow on m' face, an' I felt an arm prop up m' head. I opened m' eyes an' saw a figure with the sun shinin' behind him. From his size I knew he had t' be one o' the Big Folk."

"His face were all in shadow, but he held somethin' t' m' lips an' said, 'Drink a little o' this, slowly now. Yer're in a bad way.'

"I felt a tingle go through m' body as I drank the sweet liquor. It revived me enough so's I could sit up on m' own.

" 'Now, that's better,' the stranger said, an' he smiled. 'Here's some bread, eat it slowly.'

"I wanted t' wolf it down, but I managed t' eat it nice an' slow like he said. After a bit, I told him I thought I could stand, an' he helped me up. I gave him m' hand.

"'M' name's Jeremiah Tosis,' I said, an' we shook. 'Ya saved m' life. I'm much obliged.'

" 'I'm Calvin Endria,' he said, 'and I'm from Newburgh, the village by the bay. What type of man are you, and where are you from? I know everyone in town, and I'd swear I've never set eyes on you before.'

"Now I knew I shouldn't be tellin' him all about m'self an' m' people, but he had saved m' life after all, so I said, 'I'm a dwarf, a folk what's shorter in stature from the Big Folk, but tough-like. We often live more'n five hunnert years. Minin' an' metal workin' are our chief trades. What brings ya t' the mountains?'

" 'I'm looking for a way across,' he says. 'In time, Newburgh will outgrow its current boundries, and there's nowhere to go but over the mountains or into the sea. There's another thing, too. The pirate, Sharky, will never let us go. He'll find a way to keep us paying the Tariff beyond the hundred years we agreed upon, by force, if necessary. One day, I hope to lead my people across the mountains to whatever lands lie beyond. Then we'll be beyond the reach of the pirates.'

" 'I don't know anything 'bout no Sharky,' I says, 'But ye'll never find a way across them mountains. They're too high, there ain't no way over 'em.'

"The man nodded. 'I'm not surprised. This is my third trip into the mountains and I've had no success.'

"We talked a while, an' he told me o' his days as first mate with Cap'n Sharky an' how he an' his band come t' settle by the bay. He seemed like a decent sort, an' I found I liked him. Soon I was tellin' him 'bout the Dwarf Kingdom an' even, I have t' admit," the old dwarf blushed and glanced back at Hallo, " 'bout the Forbidden Door an' the legend o' the Jewel o' Paradise.

"He got very excited an' asked me t' take him t' King Rufus t' get permission t' go through the Door. I told him I would, but that I were lost. I described the look o' the canyon an' the wall where Side Gate were.

"Cal burst out laughin'. 'I know the spot,' he said. 'I actually followed that path into the canyon last year. I came to the wall and cursed it, thinking I'd run into a dead end.'

"I wanted t' head back right away, but he insisted on goin' back t' the village t' get more supplies."

"I waited in the hills with the little food and drink he had while he went back. The town were called Newburgh then, as I said before. Cal said he were buildin' a house at the head o' the Green, though it were just a shell at the time."

"That's my house," Kate exclaimed. "It was still being built when Cal Endria left on his final expedition."

"Cal returned the next day, an' he an' I left for the Dwarf Kingdom. I opened the Gate an' we went inside."

"Just like Hallo did with us," Eric said.

The old dwarf's face went crimson. "No, not just like him," he stammered, glancing back at Hallo. "Cal saved m' life; that makes all the difference."

"Yeah, but we saved Hallo," Eric grinned. "Isn't that so, Hallo?"

" 'Tis true, 'tis true," Hallo smiled for the first time since his father had appeared, and nodded. "I'd be dead sure without yer help, don't ya know."

"Mmm," Jeremiah grumbled, "That may be so, but it's neither here nor there. I weren't exiled. I brought him in 'cause I thought it best. 'Course, we was taken prisoner right away by a party led by m' pappy, which was on their way out t' continue the search for me.

"Naturally," Jeremiah shot a sharp look back at his son, "M' pappy were right angry 'bout me bringin' one o' the Big Folk inta the Kingdom, but he were awful grateful t' Cal for savin' m' life, too.

"It was decided I was t' be taken before the King t' be judged. Cal were t' have his case heard, too. I knew I could be banished an' prob'ly would for what I'd done—leavin' the Kingdom without the King's say-so and bringin' an outsider in t' boot—but I hoped t' be sent along with m' friend. Ya see, in them days I had an unhealthy thirst for adventure that came from bein' too young t' have sense.

"'Course, I were assumin' Cal'd be allowed t' pass beyond the Door. Most likely, though, he'd be jailed or killed.

"Well, they took us t' the King quick as anythin'. Now old King Rufus were a hard one, but he were fair. He weren't known for wisdom, but it seems t' me he had at least an av'rage share, 'cause he sent Cal on his way through the Door, but commanded that I stay behind. 'Twere the wise thing t' do, I see now. Chances were, Cal would never be seen agin an' wouldn't be talkin' t' anyone 'bout the Kingdom, an' the King weren't 'bout t' risk one o' his people on a daft journey.

"At the time, though, I couldn't see sense. I begged an' pleaded with King Rufus, but he wouldn't hear none o' it. So I determined t' go anyways—t' follow the King an' his guards when they brought Cal t' the Door. I were willin' t' fight m' way through them t' go with m' friend if need be.

"M' pappy could tell what were in m' head, an' had me tied up an' locked in the jail 'til the king an' his party had taken Cal t' the Door an' returned. So I were never able t' go with Cal on his journey. 'Course, now I know it were a good thing. Cal never did come back, an' I can only guess he met his end in the Shadowlands beyond the Door," Jeremiah sighed and shook his head.

"Do you ever wish you had been able to go with him?" Eric asked.

The old dwarf frowned as he walked. "Every so often, I feel a little sad. Could be I could've helped Cal in some way. I like t' think that, mebbe he made it through the Shadowlands t' some country beyond an' then couldn't get back. I do wonder 'bout that. I wonder what become o' him most ev'ry day."

The party continued on in silence. Hallo's brow was furrowed as he trudged behind his father.

CHAPTER 21

STONEDEEP

Within an hour, the party stood before the arched entrance
to Stonedeep. Another Imperial Captain wearing the Red
Mail greeted Jeremiah with a salute.

"Mornin', m'Lord," he said.

"Mornin', Cap'n Thrimble," Jeremiah said and continued past.

"Er, um, sorry to bother ya, m'Lord, but where're ya takin'
them?" He pointed at the rest of the group.

"Well, I was bringin' 'em inta the capitol."

"I'm 'fraid ya cain't do that, sir," Captain Thrimble gestured to a
party of guards, who blocked the group's path.

"Why on earth not?" Jeremiah's eyes grew flinty.

"Well, sir, meanin' no disrespect," the captain fiddled with his
beard, "but them's two's Big Folk, undesirables, an' that bird don't
have no license."

"Ya dolt! Theys under m' protection," Jeremiah roared, his face
red. "We got a' audience with the King t'day!"

"Beg pardon, beg pardon," Captain Thrimble fawned. "I'll jest
check the ledger if ya don't mind. 'Taint personal, ya understand, jest
regulation."

Thrimble barked a command to a black-bearded guard, who scurried to the guardhouse and returned in an instant with a large book bound in black leather. The Captain paged through it.

"Hmm, let's see, um, ah...oh yeah, here we are. Royal Goldsmithy an' party t' be received 8:30 in the palace. Well, go on through, ye're clear t' pass. Good luck with yer business, m'Lord. 'Tweren't anythin' personal, ya understand, jest regulation," the Captain apologized as he waved them on.

"Hmm," Jeremiah rumbled as he led them past, "seems a little common sense should temper them regulations."

With that, they passed under the arch and into Stonedeep. Eric saw at once that it was grander than any other town he'd seen in the Dwarf Kingdom. The entry arch was huge—Eric thought at least 50 feet wide and 100 feet high. The wall into which the arch was cut was carved with countless figures of dwarves covered in gold and clad in jewels that sparkled and glowed.

Inside, the cavern that housed Stonedeep was so huge, Eric could barely see the other side. From what he could see, the walls of the cavern were full of tier upon tier of government offices, all with vine and flower gardens. The floor of the city was filled with buildings and the tents of merchants as in the other towns, but their wares were more exotic. Pushy, talkative merchants shouted the benefits of their wares to the thousands of dwarf tourists who had come to view the wonders of their capital. From over to his left, Eric heard a dull roar. Looking in that direction, he saw a huge waterfall—a sheet of water tumbling and cascading down into a pool in a rear corner of the cavern. He looked up to find the waterfall's source, and saw that it issued from the mouth of a cave in the wall high above.

"Wow." He'd never seen such an awesome sight.

"It's so beautiful," said Kate. "It makes Tumbledown Falls look like a fountain."

"I say," Stig almost forgot to keep flapping his wings, "it's magnificent. This cavern doesn't seem to end. There's no ceiling that I can see."

Eric realized Stig was right. Above the dwellings on the cavern walls, he saw glowmoss growing. But when he looked straight up, beyond the reach of the light from the glowmoss, he saw nothing but darkness.

Jeremiah noticed the children and the owl staring around them with wonder. "When our forefathers first built the Kingdom," he said, "they placed Stonedeep under the tallest o' the Iron Mountains—ol' Misty Top. They spent the next two hunnert years hollowin' it out 'til it weren't no more'n a shell. As ya kin see, it feels almost like we're outside. There's windows up there, so that in the daytime, there's lots o' natural light streamin' down. Ye'll see it soon, dawn ain't no more'n a few minutes away."

As they walked, Eric noticed it was getting progressively lighter. By the time they were halfway across the floor of the city, the cavern was full of natural sunlight streaming down from the unseen reaches above.

Eric hadn't realized how long it had been since he'd felt sunlight on his face, nor how much he'd missed it. It lightened his heart and gave him hope. He felt like laughing out loud. Kate and Stig were feeling much the same way, if their smiles and bright eyes were any indication.

The natural beauty of the plants, the waterfall and the sunlight weren't Stonedeep's only assets, however. Eric saw that the main road was lined with golden statues on jewel-encrusted pedestals, just as in Silverlode. As they neared the palace, he saw that its marble walls were covered with more of the intricate reliefs they'd seen all over the kingdom. Here, though, they were gilded in silver and gold.

The palace was built into the center of the far wall of the cavern. It was a long rectangle fronted with pillars of red marble that held up a massive peaked roof of pale-blue quartz. Steps led up to the pillars. It looked, Eric thought, like the Lincoln Memorial, only bigger and more breathtaking.

Jeremiah led them up the steps to the entrance. It was guarded by more imperial soldiers in the Red Mail. They were expected. The soldiers saluted them and ushered them into the palace.

The interior was every bit as grand as the outside. The entrance hall had a high vaulted ceiling supported by two rows of thin, almost delicate columns made of a silvery metal. They were wrought to look like tree trunks, fanning out at the top like branches spreading across the ceiling, which was fashioned from a green metal, hammered to look like leaves. The white marble floors were streaked with pale grays, blues, greens and reds that Eric found pleasing. The columns formed an aisle that led the length of the palace. Between each pillar on either side of the hall was a great golden door. From time to time a dwarf would come out of one door, and move down the hall to enter another.

They were greeted by a red-bearded dwarf. He wore a red cap, bright-blue tunic, white breeches and knee-high black boots that were polished and shiny. He took off his cap and bowed until his beard touched the floor.

"I'm the King's chamberlain, Jenks," he said, "ye're t' come with me t' the throne room."

"Jenks, what're we s'posed t' do with him," Jeremiah jerked his thumb over his shoulder at Hallo. "He's a' outcast ya know."

The Chamberlain peered at Hallo down his nose as he spoke to Jeremiah. "I know, m'Lord, the King says t' make an 'ception an' bring him too."

Jenks led them down the hall. As they walked, Eric heard the sound of water splashing. In the center of the palace, the corridor they were following intersected with another. In the center of the intersection stood a large silver fountain that bubbled and tinkled. Eric was fascinated by it, because it was an exact replica of the waterfall in Stonedeep.

They circled around and continued on. After another few minutes, the hallway ended in front of a large gold door. Imperial Guardsmen stood on either side. They opened the doors, and Jenks led them inside.

The room was smaller than Eric had expected, given the grand nature of the palace. He guessed it was smaller than his school's auditorium. It was decorated in the same manner as the hall, with tree-like silvery pillars and the green metal leaf ceiling. The wall at the far end of the room, however, took Eric's breath away. It was clad in a magnificent jeweled fresco depicting a golden sun, its rays blazing forth in all directions, against a brilliant blue sky. Marble stairs led to a dais on which stood a red-cushioned throne of gold.

Seated on the throne was King Angus Thunderhelm. His brown beard was braided with gold. King Angus wore a red doublet and cream-colored breeches. He wore black leather boots that came to the knee. A large battleaxe was laid across his knees.

The crown on his head was fashioned of gold in the shape of an eagle's head. Its beak curved down to cover and protect the king's nose. Two large blue sapphires were set in the head for eyes, and diamonds, rubies and emeralds circled the crown's base. The eagle's feathers were highlighted with silver.

"Royal Goldsmithy," King Angus beckoned him. "Step forward."

"Yes, yer Majesty," Jeremiah took off his cap, stepped forward and bowed low.

"What did ya want t' see me 'bout, Jeremiah?" the King asked. "And who're yer friends? Looks like ya got two young outsiders with ya."

"Well, sir, that's what I'm here 'bout, actually." Jeremiah twisted his cap in his hand.

"I s'pose yer gonna tell me how it is they got int' the Kingdom. They must've had some help. Ya didn't let 'em in, did ya?" the King said, and frowned.

"No sir, yer Majesty." Eric was surprised at how meek the crusty old dwarf had become. Jeremiah seemed to be trembling. "I didn't let 'em in. My, er...um, son...or rather an exiled dwarf brought 'em in t' the Kingdom."

The King's eyes bored a hole into Jeremiah. "Let me get the straight o' this," King Angus said with a low growl that rose to a bellow. "Do ya mean t' say that yer exiled no-account son let the Big Folk in?"

"Er, um ya might say that, in a manner o' speakin', yer Majesty," Jeremiah said. "But I spoke t' the children an' the bird, an' I believe there was good reason."

"Spoke t' the bird?" the King roared. "Are ya daft or do ya take me for a fool, Jeremiah?"

"No, sir, it ain't neither o' them things," Jeremiah lifted his head. "The lass is direct kin t' Cal Endria. Her village is in trouble, an' she, the lad an' the bird have come t' ask for yer help."

"The bird, Jeremiah?" The King squinted at the old dwarf. "Yer a fine hand with gold, old friend, but p'rhaps yer mind's come unhinged jest a bit."

"Oh no, sir," said Jeremiah who looked back over his shoulder. "Ya can talk, can't ya, bird?"

"Most assuredly," Stig replied. "Though His Majesty might not believe it, I've been talking practically all my life. However, I don't think that's so important just now. We need the help of the Dwarf Kingdom to defeat the pirates. There's really no time to waste."

King Angus gaped for a moment. Then he shut his mouth and frowned. "Hmmm," he said. "Lass, come forward an' tell me what's goin' on in yer village."

So Kate stepped forward and told the King about the history of her village, from Cal Endria's deal with Sharky to the arrival of Eric and Stig and the attack of the pirates. When she had finished, the King pursed his lips and stroked his beard.

"Lad, come here." He gestured to Eric, who approached the throne with Stig. "Is it true yer not of this world?"

"Yes, your Majesty, that's true. Stig and I were sent to help Calendria with its problem. I guess we're not doing a very good job. Things haven't been going so well."

"Sometimes these things get worse before they get better," Stig said.

"Well, that's a tale an' no mistake," the king said. "I'll have t' think on this. Jenks, take these folks an' give 'em somethin' t' eat while I chew this over."

Jenks led them out of the throne room through a side door into a small antechamber that was just big enough to hold benches and a stone table laden with food. When Jenks was assured they had everything they needed, he left them to their meal. With nothing else to do, they ate, talked and waited for King Angus to come to a decision.

After what seemed a long time to Eric, Jenks returned and ushered them back into the throne room.

King Angus sat on the throne, his brow still furrowed in thought. For all Eric could tell, the king hadn't moved a muscle the entire time. The group stood before the throne and waited without a word.

"Come closer, the lot o' ya." King Angus rose and gestured to them to come to the foot of the dais. "I've given yer story a bit o' thought. Lass," he said to Kate, "it's a tough spot for yer people t' be in, that's for sure. I sympathize with yer troubles, but I'm not too keen t' risk m' folk without some sort o' reward."

"I'm sure my Father and the Council would be willing to pay you for your help, Your Majesty," Kate said.

"Unfortunately, I don't think there's anythin' ya have that we need, lass," the King replied. "However, there's one thing we need that per'aps one o' ya could get."

"What's that?" asked Kate.

"One o' ya just may be the one t' get us the Jewel o' Paradise." The King looked at Eric as he spoke.

"You mean me, don't you, sir?" Eric asked.

"Yer familiar with the legend?" asked the King, somewhat surprised.

"Yeah, Hallo told us about it," Eric said, then realized his mistake.

King Angus, seeming to notice the outcast dwarf for the first time, looked at Hallo with some disapproval. "That's somethin' no dwarf should speak of t' outsiders without the King's approval," said King Angus. Jeremiah shot a quick look at Hallo, his face red with embarrassment. "But that don't matter right now. In fact, it could help. Since ya know the legend, then ya know the Jewel can be won only by an outsider. M' pappy thought that mebbe Cal Endria bein'

139

an outsider might be the one t' win it, but he were wrong. I'm thinkin' mebbe someone from outside the world is the one t' win it."

"What are you saying, Your Majesty?" Stig asked.

"Just this. If both of ya go through the Forbidden Door an' bring back the Jewel, then I'll send m' army t' rid Calendria o' the pirates once an' for all. That's m' deal; take it or leave it."

Eric looked at Stig, then at Kate. The owl's golden eyes were calm. Kate's eyes pleaded with him.

Eric took a deep breath, then said, "We'll go through the Door."

"I want to go too!" Kate demanded.

"I can't send ya, lass," the King said.

"Why not?" Kate asked. "I'm an outsider, too. It's my village, after all. I'm not going to be left behind!"

King Angus stroked his beard. "All right, if ya have yer heart set on it, ya can go."

Kate clapped her hands and hugged Eric. Eric smiled, his happiness that Kate and Stig would be going with him overshadowing his nervousness. Then, he remembered Hallo.

The dwarf stood alone a few yards behind them. Jeremiah stood in between, his back to his son. Hallo stared at his father's back, a look of anguish on his face.

The boy turned back to the throne. "Your Majesty, what's going to happen to Hallo?"

"What? Oh, er, um, he's outcast. To return to the Kingdom is death. After ya leave, he'll be executed."

"Well, I was thinking, your Majesty," Eric said, "Hallo's been exiled, so that means he's not part of the Dwarf Kingdom, right?"

"Aye, lad. An exiled dwarf has no place in the Kingdom," the king said.

"Well, doesn't that make him an outsider, too?" Eric asked. "Couldn't you send him with us?"

"Er, um, well now." The king frowned. "I don't rightly know. It ain't the law. Still, ain't no one come back through the Forbidden Door." The king gestured to Hallo. "Come here, you."

Hallo joined the children and the owl at the foot of the dais. "Yes, yer Majesty," he said, bowing low.

"Yer an outcast, but I'm givin' ya a chance," the king said. "Ya can go through the Forbidden Door with these outsiders in search o' the Jewel, or ya can stay an' be executed. Which'll it be?"

"I'll go through the Door, yer Majesty," Hallo said, grinning. "An' thank'ee, yer Majesty."

"Right, now that's settled, let's go." King Angus rose from his throne and walked down the dais steps.

Jenks appeared and gave each of them a knapsack. "I've had Jenks prepare some provisions for yer journey," said the king. "Some rations, water, glowmoss torches, hotstones an' a measure o' black powder for each o' ya."

King Angus led them out a small door beside the dais. Jeremiah followed them, but Jenks remained behind.

Eric and the others followed the king through the door into a narrow stone passage lit by glowmoss. The dusty, cobweb-strewn passage ran for a little way before ending at a flat stone wall, which Eric knew wasn't a wall.

King Angus stopped and addressed them. "This is the Forbidden Door," he said. "It's goin' t' be dark when ya go through. In your packs you'll find torches made with glowmoss."

They rummaged through their packs until they found their torches and pulled them out.

"Is everyone ready?" asked the king. They nodded. "Good, then I'll open the door."

The king raised his left hand palm outward in the same gesture Eric had seen Hallo use on the Side Door. King Angus pressed the palm of his hand to the door, and it ground open.

"Good luck to all o' ya," the king said. He gave a slight smile and stood aside to let them pass through.

Eric, Kate and Stig went into the darkness beyond. Hallo was crossing the threshold when Jeremiah rushed after him with a sob. The old dwarf grabbed his son in a rough embrace.

"Good luck, son." His voice was harsh, but there were tears in his eyes. "Take care o' yerself."

"I'll do m' best, Pap," Hallo's eyes were moist, too. Then he turned and walked through the Door.

"An' don't foul it up!" Jeremiah yelled as the Forbidden Door closed with a dull boom.

CHAPTER 22

DEFENSE

The villagers of Calendria held on. Sharky and his men, unable to fight their way through the defenders at the top of the hill, had regrouped at the harbor. The ships in the bay fired their cannon, trying to batter the villagers into submission. While most of the buildings on the Green were undamaged, the houses on Main Avenue were all destroyed.

Under the direction of Cordon and Mr. Flint, the villagers had built a barricade of stone at the top of Main Avenue just below the Green. It bristled with the sharp iron spikes that were to have been part of the chain across the harbor. They stuck out from the wall like the quills of a porcupine. So far, Nan and her archers had turned back every pirate charge.

From behind the wall, the Lord Mayor surveyed the situation with Cordon and Madame Bottleneck. As he looked out over the destruction of the lower village, he wondered how much longer the brave townsfolk could hold out.

"What's their next move, I wonder?" he thought out loud.

"They just might give up and go home," said Madame Bottleneck. "We've stood up to them. I doubt anyone's ever tested them this way. A surprise attack and quick surrender's what they're used to."

"Could be, but I doubt it," Cordon said, and shook his head, his black ponytail waving from side to side. "We've challenged 'em and hurt their pride, not to mention sunk some ships and killed some of their men. They won't rest until we're wiped out."

"Cordon's right, I'm afraid," the Lord Mayor said. "This is going to be a fight to the death if they have their way. Our only chance is that Kate and the others bring back help from the dwarves."

Cordon spat on the ground. "That's not much of one," he said. "They've spent too many years hiding under the mountains to stick their necks out now."

"That's not fair, Cordon," Madame Bottleneck said, turning to the smith. "Hallo's a very decent person. I'm sure the rest are, too."

"Yeah, but they kicked him out," Cordon said. "Maybe they don't want any decent folk."

"Okay, that's enough," the Lord Mayor said. "Unfortunately, I think Cordon's right. Chances are slim that we'll get help from the dwarves. Still, some hope is better than none at all. We have to make sure we hold out as long as possible to give Kate, Eric, Hallo and Stig enough time to at least reach the king and ask."

"I'll put Flint and some of the farmers to work extending the wall so those scum can't outflank us." Cordon pointed at the rubble strewn hillside. "It's tough going, picking a path through that, but they'll probably try that next. I think they're finding out a frontal attack is suicide."

"Right," said the Lord Mayor. "Do that, then. Whatever happens, they must not get up on the Green. If they get around behind us, we're finished."

Cordon strode off to find Mr. Flint.

"Do you think we'll be able to hold them off, Charles?" Madame Bottleneck asked.

"I don't know, Moira." The Lord Mayor frowned. "We may, for a time. But we'll fall eventually. The only way to win is to kill them all or drive them off and, right now, we don't have a way to do that."

They were joined by Mrs. Casker. The chubby woman wore a white shirt, a blue skirt and a worn leather apron. Her short, sandy-blond hair was touched with gray, and she wore a pair of wire-rimmed glasses. Although she was as tired as the rest of the defenders, her rosy cheeks and ever-present smile hid that. Her cheery brown eyes were thoughtful.

"Charles, I've just had an idea," she said.

"Yes, Dolores?" the Lord Mayor asked.

"Well, I just passed Cordon, and he told me we have to defend the Green at all costs," she said.

"Yes, that's right."

"Well, I've got a lot of barrels in my shop, and I thought maybe we could use them in the defense."

"You mean, fill them with dirt and use them as a barricade?" the Lord Mayor scratched his beard. "That could work."

"Well, that's a good idea, too," Mrs. Casker said. "But I was thinking of filling them with rocks and metal and black powder. Then we could set them on fire and roll them down the hill. It may keep them from marching up the hill again. If we're lucky, a few might even make it into their camp. That would really disrupt things, wouldn't it?"

The Lord Mayor and Madame Bottleneck smiled at the little round woman. "It certainly would, Dolores, it certainly would," the Lord Mayor said, giving her a big hug.

CHAPTER 23

BEYOND

They were in a small cavern. Eric could hear the echo of water dripping in the distance. The torches gave off a faint light that barely kept the inky blackness at bay. The air in the cavern was cool. A slight breeze made Eric shiver.

"It's chilly." Kate's voice seemed loud and harsh as it echoed off the walls.

"It's a bleak sort o' place, don't ya know," said Hallo. "I'm thinkin' we best be movin' on."

"Yeah, but which way?" asked Eric. "How big is this cavern?"

"I'll fly out and check," Stig said. His golden eyes sparkled in the light of the torches. "I can see very nicely in the dark, so long as there aren't any torches to blind me. I'll be back in a moment." The owl flew off.

It was hard for Eric to tell how long Stig was gone, but it seemed like a long time. Kate and Eric were both starting to shiver and Hallo was shuffling from foot to foot when the owl returned.

"The cavern's quite large," he said, "and the only exit is on the opposite side—a tunnel in the rock. About twenty yards from here the ground on the right drops off rather suddenly to form a cliff. You'll have to follow me to avoid falling in."

They set out with Stig in the lead, followed by Eric, Kate and Hallo.

"Is the tunnel natural?" asked Eric as they walked.

"It's hard to say for certain," said Stig, "but it looks man-made to me."

"Ya mean dwarf-made, don't ya?" Hallo corrected.

"I say, I suppose you're right."

"Are there people here, do you think?" Kate asked.

"There ain't no one here," Hallo's voice was bleak. "Even m' pappy, who had me exiled an' wouldn't talk t' me this whole time, even he broke down when I got sent through the Door. For dwarves, it's like a death sentence, don't ya know."

"So King Angus didn't really want to help us; he was just getting rid of us," Eric said.

"Well that may be true, and it may not be. See, it's true none's ever come back, but it's also true that only an outsider can get the Jewel. So I'm a thinkin' the king is half hopin' we do it. If we fail, he ain't lost nothin'. If we bring back the Jewel, the Kingdom will be sure t' get some benefit."

"The tunnel is just up ahead," Stig called back. "I'm flying in now."

They came to the tunnel and followed the owl inside. It was only about six feet high and only two could walk abreast. Stig continued to fly ahead, followed by Hallo and then Eric and Kate walking side by side. The tunnel was not straight. It curved first left, then right, then left again. After following it for a little bit, Eric could no longer tell what direction he was going.

The tunnel began to slope downward. Eric noticed that the air in the tunnel was becoming warmer, and a slight breeze held a sulphurous smell.

"There's a light up ahead," said Stig.

But the owl didn't have to tell them. Eric could see an eerie reddish glow flickering ahead of them. The passage continued to descend, and the light got stronger. They put away their torches and crept forward.

Eric and the others joined the owl at a bend in the tunnel. From there, they moved on together. After one more turn, the passage opened to the outside. At least that's what Eric thought. The reddish light was stronger now, but there was a thick fog, which made it impossible for him to make out anything beyond the opening.

"What do we do now?" Kate whispered.

"We've got t' go out there, don't ya know," Hallo said. "It's what we come for."

"Yeah," Eric took a deep breath. "Let's go."

He crept out of the tunnel into the fog. The others followed. It was hard to see anything. Eric looked up to the sky. He could not see the sun, just the brooding reddish glow.

A warm breeze hit them as they emerged. It made Eric's skin feel clammy. A creaking, rattling noise came from the mist somewhere ahead. Eric stopped short and the others came to a halt behind him. To him, the noise sounded like rattling bones.

Eric peered into the murk, and thought he could see a dark mass rising in front of him. He took a deep breath.

"I think there's something up ahead," he said. "Come on, you guys."

They started forward again, Stig flying beside Eric.

"I can't see anything in this fog," the boy said to the owl.

All at once, the fog parted. They found themselves at the edge of a forest. Huge gnarled trees bristled, their bark cracked and gray.

Eric looked up and saw that the trees were dead. Their branches loomed over them like bony fingers.

"I wonder how big this forest is," he said.

"I'll fly up and have a look around," said Stig, and flew off into the gloom.

In a few minutes, he was back. "Not very much to report," he said. "The fog is thick everywhere but here. As near as I can tell, the forest is huge. It spreads from the feet of the mountains out into the fog. The strange part is, all the trees are dead."

"So we can't walk around it?" Eric asked.

"Not very likely," Stig shook his head. "Mind you, it was hard to tell for sure in the fog, but the forest seems to stretch in every direction."

"We'll have to go through it then," Eric said.

"It would seem so," said Stig. "Oh, one other thing. The red glow looks like it's coming from a source high up in the sky beyond the forest."

"Isn't it the sun?" Kate asked.

"It may be," Stig frowned, "But it's too red."

"Maybe the fog makes it seem that way," said Kate.

"You could be right, but I've a feeling it's something else," Stig said.

"Could be the Jewel, don't ya know," said Hallo looking thoughtful.

"The Jewel?" Eric asked. "What makes you think so?"

"It's another part o' the legend." Hallo tugged at his ear and squinted at the sky. "Lemme see. Oh yeah, the legend says that the Jewel will burn with a red fire 'til the hero sets his hand on it. When he tames it, it'll glow with the color o' paradise, don't ya know."

Eric shivered. The only thing the red glow in the sky reminded him of was the red glow in the mist of his dream. He shook his head and peered into the forest.

"We better get going," he said. The rest nodded their agreement, and together they went in.

The trees must be so close they keep out the breeze, Eric thought, for as soon as they passed into the forest, the air became still, although the branches overhead continued to creak.

The fog was unable to penetrate, either. It was clear and dark. Eric, Kate and Hallo took out their glowmoss torches. The faint glow from the torches lit only a small area around them. The darkness of the forest hung like a blanket a few feet above their heads. When Eric looked up, it seemed the trees were hovering over them, reaching down with their branches to engulf them. A feeling of fear gripped him.

As they trudged through the forest, the fear grew. The looks on the faces of his companions told Eric he wasn't the only one who was afraid. How long they walked in the never-ending gloom, he couldn't tell. Every so often, Stig would fly up above the forest to make sure they were traveling in a straight line toward what they thought was the source of the red light. Eric didn't like it, but it was the only thing they had to steer by.

When they felt they could not go any further, they sat down and had something to eat. Then they put their torches away, wrapped themselves up in their blankets, and went to sleep. Stig slept on a low-hanging branch.

Eric awoke to inky blackness, the dry smell of the dead forest and the same feeling of fear. He guessed he'd gotten a full night's sleep, but couldn't tell with the lack of light. He pulled his torch out of his pack. Its light seemed feeble in the unnatural darkness, but it was enough for him to make out the sleeping forms of Kate and Hallo.

"Hey, you guys, wake up," he whispered. "We got to get going."

Kate stirred, but Hallo continued to snore. Eric got up and prodded the dwarf with his sneaker, as Kate sat up.

"Is it morning already?" she asked, rubbing the sleep from her violet eyes.

"Might be," Eric said as he put away his blanket. "Hard to tell, though."

"It feels like morning," Stig said from the branch above them.

"How can ya tell?" Hallo asked. He was still wrapped in his blanket. With his head and long red beard poking out of one end, Eric thought he looked like a caterpillar that had stopped weaving its cocoon too soon.

"Oh, owls can tell," Stig said. "It's what you might call instinct."

"If ya say so," Hallo scratched his head. "Might as well be mornin' as any other time o' day."

They ate a quick, cold breakfast and broke camp. The glowmoss torches lit their way, and Stig kept them on course toward the reddish light.

The forest never seemed to change, and Stig reported he still could not see its end. Eric was beginning to think it would go on forever, when the owl returned from scouting later that day.

"There's a clearing up ahead," he told them.

"How far?" Eric asked.

"Not very," Stig replied. "I should think we'll reach it shortly."

Intrigued, the little group quickened its pace. Eric was anxious for a break in what had become a boring routine.

After a bit, the trees came to an abrupt end and Eric and his friends found themselves in a large clearing. The lack of trees let in the dull red light. In that light, Eric was able to see that the clearing had once been home to a small settlement. Twelve foundations of stone, worn by time, were set in a circle. Heaps of rubble lay in the dust—all that remained of the walls, he guessed.

"What do you suppose all this is?" Stig waved a wing to indicate the ruins.

"It looks like an old village," Eric said.

"It's the first sign of life we've seen here," Stig said, and frowned. "I wonder what happened to the villagers."

"Must've high-tailed it out o' here," Hallo said. "Can't say as I blame 'em. This here ain't my idea o' a nice neighborhood, don't ya know."

The dwarf knelt to examine the cracked and weathered stone. "This ain't dwarf work, that's sure," he said. "It ain't half bad, though."

"What do you think happened to the buildings, Hallo?" Eric asked.

"If ya ask me, it looks like they were knocked down, don't ya know," the dwarf said.

While the other three had been examining the stones, Kate had wandered into the center of the circle.

"Hey, you guys!" she called. "Come here and look at this!"

The others came over to where she crouched. As he came up, Eric could see that she was holding her torch close to something on the ground. He thought he saw a glint of gold.

Kate reached down and picked up what looked like an old book. The others gathered around her. It was indeed a book, its leather cover weather-stained and cracked with age. A leather strap with a brass clasp held the book shut.

"It looks like a diary," Eric said.

Kate's eyes were alight. "It's a journal!"

"I say, do you think it could be Cal Endria's personal journal?" Stig asked.

"There's only one way t' find out, don't ya know," Hallo said.

"Yeah," Eric said. "Open it, Kate."

Kate undid the clasp and opened the book. Its pages were brittle and covered with a faded, flowing script. The others crowded behind Kate and looked over her shoulders. Hallo and Eric held their torches over her to give her some more light.

"I can't read much," Kate said, squinting.

"Okay, then let's build a fire," Eric said. "There's plenty of dead wood around."

Soon they had a large fire crackling in the center of the circle. The bright light cheered them.

They put their torches away, and settled down around the fire. In the shifting light of the flames, Kate began to read. Eric felt an electricity in the air.

" 'Monday, June 14th. Had my audience with the king today. It was more like a trial. He said he'd 'decide my fate' in the morning. So, tonight, I am housed in a charming room in the palace jail. Actually, it's technically not a jail, and really is quite nice. Still, there are guards outside the door, and I'm not allowed to leave.

" 'Had a visit from Jeremiah tonight.' "

Kate looked up, a light in her eyes. "It's definitely Cal Endria's journal!" she said then continued to read.

" 'Had a visit from Jeremiah tonight. He apologized that I'd been locked up by his folk. I told him it was okay, but he shook his head and said, "No it ain't." ' "

" 'I laughed and told him not to worry. After all, I reminded him, I'd broken one of their sacred laws by coming into the Kingdom.

" 'But ya had help, didn't ya?" Jeremiah said, and a grin split his face. "B'sides, ya saved m' life. That should count for something." ' "

" 'He stopped grinning then, and his face became real serious. "I'm comin' with ya tomorrer," he said.

" 'I thanked him, but told him it wasn't necessary. He shook his head and said, "I got t' go. Like I said, ya saved m' life, an' I'm gonna stand by ya. If His Majesty sends ya beyond the Door, I'm goin' with ya." ' "

Kate stopped.

"Why'd ya stop?" Hallo snapped. He had a strange expression on his face.

"I'm sorry, Hallo," Kate said. "The rest of the page has faded." She flipped forward a few pages. "The ink's kind of spotty."

"I suppose it would be after almost three hundred years," Stig said.

"Here's something I can read," Kate peered at the book. "Hey, listen to this!"

" 'June 18th? Not sure of the day. I've been wandering in this accursed forest for days. At least it seems like days. It's always dark. The dwarves gave me a glowmoss torch, but there's no way to tell what direction I'm going. The trees here are all dead. Food and water won't last forever. I have made camp. Plenty of wood for a fire, so I built one. I'm glad I did. The flicker of flames and crackle of the wood is good company. Wish they had let Jeremiah come with me. He sure put up a fight when the king said he couldn't.

" 'He's very brave. Everybody in the throne room went stone silent when old Rufus said he was sending me beyond the Door. Jeremiah was the only one who wasn't afraid. But his father was ready for him. As soon as Jeremiah started to argue, three dwarves grabbed him. He put up a good fight, but in the end they hog-tied him and that was that.' "

As Kate read those words aloud, Eric looked at Hallo. The dwarf shook his head and muttered, "That's Pap. Guess he's always been tough as a ol' turnip." In spite of his words, the dwarf was smiling.

Kate continued to read.

" 'June 19th. I've stumbled upon an old village. Nothing much left of it but piles of rubble set in a circle, but it's a break from the endless trees. This forest is a brooding place. It feels like I'm being watched. Every so often, there's a rustling in the branches above me, although there is not a hint of wind.

" 'When I sit by the fire after a long march, it seems there are dozens of pairs of red eyes peering at me out of the darkness. The fire shines off them like the sun glinting off flecks of mica. I believe this dead forest and the darkness is causing me to take leave of my senses.'

"That's the end of the entry," Kate said. "The rest of the pages are blank."

"I wonder what he meant by eyes," Eric mused.

"I don't know," Kate frowned. "We haven't seen anything so far."

"I've seen nothing lurking in the treetops on my scouting missions," Stig said.

"A lot of things can change in three hundred years. It could be there were strange creatures here back then, but maybe they've died off by now. I mean, there used to be some sort of civilization here." Eric waved his arms to indicate the ruins. "They seem to have died or moved on even before Cal Endria's time. It might be the same with the creatures he wrote about."

"I don't know," Hallo glanced up at the trees and the red glow in the sky. "This forest seems unnatural somehow, don't ya know. The whole place seems dead. We ain't seen nothin' alive since we went beyond the Door. B'sides, what happened t' Cal Endria t' make him leave his journal? He must've left right quick t' forget somethin' like that. I'm a-thinkin' it might be Bolliwogs."

No one had an answer to that. Stig shifted his weight from foot to foot, and Kate kept glancing up at the lifeless trees. Eric felt a little uneasy himself. All of a sudden, he thought he heard a rustling in the treetops at the far edge of the clearing.

He shook his head, thinking he was letting his imagination run away with him. One look at the others, though, told him that they had heard something as well.

"Did you hear that?" Kate's voice quivered.

"I think so," Hallo replied.

Eric and Stig nodded.

"It's coming from over there," Eric pointed across the clearing.

"I do believe you're right," Stig said.

"What are we going to do about it?" Kate asked.

"Well, whatever we do, we mustn't panic," Stig said. "We can't show that we're afraid."

"W-who's afraid?" Kate asked.

"I sure as heck am," Hallo said. "There's somethin' out there. If they're anythin' like the rest o' this place, they ain't gonna be too nice, I'm a-thinkin.'"

While the others had been talking, Eric had been watching the trees across the clearing. Now, he jumped to his feet. "Hey, guys," he pointed toward the trees, "look."

From just beyond the light of the fire, they could see dozens of pairs of red eyes watching them.

CHAPTER 24

THE MOUNTAIN

E verybody stopped and stared, wide-eyed.
"What are they?" Eric asked.

"I don't know, but I'm a-thinkin' they ain't lookin' t' make friends," Hallo said.

Just then, a noise like the whoosh of air from a giant bellows rose from the forest. Into the circle swarmed dozens of huge bats. Their fierce eyes were red, and green poison dripped from their yellow fangs.

"Bats!" Eric yelled.

"Not bats, it's th' Bolliwogs!" Hallo yelled, his eyes filled with fear. "Grab yer gear an' run!"

"I'll hang back and try to hold them off," Stig said.

"I'll help ya," Hallo said, and pulled a burning branch from the fire.

Stig flew headlong into the bats, scattering them. Hallo ran after him, waving the burning stick over his head. As he ran, he looked back at the two children. "Go!" he yelled, "We'll catch up!"

Eric and Kate picked up the packs and ran from the clearing. They crashed through the forest for a while before they stopped, panting. They listened for sounds of pursuit, but heard none.

Eric pulled two glowmoss torches from the packs. "We'd better get going," he said and handed one of the torches to Kate.

"What about Stig and Hallo?" Kate asked.

"Stig will find us," Eric said. "He's at home in the dark."

They proceeded with caution. Eric felt as if he'd been going forever when he heard a noise in the forest behind them. He stopped and gestured to Kate to do the same. They both put away their torches and waited in the darkness.

The noise became louder. Then Eric heard the sound of beating wings, and his blood froze.

"I say, it's only me," Stig said, and landed on the ground beside them.

Eric released his breath with a whoosh. He hadn't even realized he'd been holding it as he crouched. He felt as if his lungs were about to burst. "Stig, you scared me half to death! Where's Hallo?"

"He's right behind," Stig said. "He should be along presently."

"What happened?" Kate asked.

"We threw them into a bit of confusion back there," Stig chuckled. "But I don't know if it will be enough to throw them off our trail."

"Then as soon as Hallo gets here, we'd better get going," Eric said.

Just then, Hallo came running up. He still held what was left of the burning branch, now just a stump smoldering in his hand.

"They're a-comin' up behind, don't ya know," he gasped. "They're still a ways back, but we'd better get a move on all the same."

Eric gave Hallo a torch, and the dwarf discarded the branch. With Stig leading the way, they started off.

For a while, all was quiet. After they'd been traveling for a bit, though, Eric thought he could hear the faint sounds of the pursuing Bolliwogs. As they went, those sounds became louder and they were forced to put their torches away and run through the darkness.

Stig dropped back a couple of times to slow down the Bolli-wogs. Judging from the increasing noise behind them, it was obvious to Eric that the owl's efforts were becoming less and less successful.

After his latest foray, Stig flew beside Eric as the boy ran. "I'm going to fly ahead," Stig said. "Perhaps I can find some place for us to hide."

Eric nodded, and the owl flew off. The boy was too tired to do anything but run, and he knew he wouldn't be able to do that much longer. Hallo, running on his short but strong legs, looked as if he could go on forever, but it was clear to Eric that Kate was as tired as he was.

Eric was relieved when Stig returned only a few minutes later. "I've found a place up ahead!" he called, loud enough for the other three to hear him. "I'll lead you there; it's not far!"

They followed the owl to a massive hollow tree. Eric could see a large opening at its base. He bent down and scrambled in, followed by Kate, Hallo and Stig. Once inside, they sat in the dark interior of the tree, gasping for breath. It smelled of rot.

As he sat gulping air, Eric listened for the sound of wings. It wasn't long before he heard them. He held his breath in an effort to keep silent, and he noticed that Kate and Hallo did, too. They listened as the rush of wings passed over them and faded into the distance.

Eric breathed a sigh of relief as he pulled his torch out of his pack and looked at his friends. Their faces, though still tense, looked relieved as well.

"What now?" Kate whispered.

"We're never gonna get anywhere 'til we get out of this forest," Eric said.

"Aye, it ain't healthy, don't ya know," Hallo said. "But the thing is, how in heck do we do that?"

"I'm going to scout around a little. The far edge of the forest can't be very far off. You may not have noticed down here, but up above the forest, the red light is getting stronger. That must mean the edge is near. I'll be back as soon as I can. Everyone try to get some sleep while I'm gone," Stig said, then flew off.

After Stig had gone, the others settled down for a bite to eat and some sleep. When Eric awoke, he saw that Stig had returned. The white owl was asleep, his head tucked under his wing. Eric decided to wait for a while before waking him.

When Stig and the others had woken up, Eric asked, "Any hope?"

"Well, yes and no," the owl replied.

"What do you mean?" Kate frowned.

"Actually, we're quite close to the edge of the forest," Stig said. "It's about a half-hour's march from here, less if you run. There's a huge mountain just beyond the forest's edge. It appears the red light is coming from the top."

"So what's the bad news?" Eric asked. The news about a mountain filled him with a feeling of foreboding.

"The Bolliwogs are sitting in the trees along the edge of the forest," Stig said. "They must have realized they missed us, so they're waiting."

"For us?" Eric asked.

"Apparently," Stig replied.

Eric looked around at his friends. In the dim light from the torches, they looked pale and scared.

"So what should we do, guys?" he asked them.

"We've got to come up with a plan," Kate said.

"Aye, an' these cursed Bolliwogs ain't no dummies," Hallo said. "So it'll be a tough job, don't ya know."

They sat for a while in silence, each trying to think of a plan. Try as he might, Eric couldn't think of a thing. His thoughts kept drifting beyond the forest and the Bolliwogs to the mountain.

"Mebbe we could set fire t' the trees an' burn 'em out," Hallo suggested.

"No, no, that won't do, I'm afraid," Stig shook his head. "If we were to set the trees on fire, we wouldn't be able to get through the flames and out of the forest ourselves."

Kate sat with her brow furrowed in thought. "What if we don't set the fire at the forest's edge?" she asked.

"How do you mean?" Stig asked.

"What if you all go on ahead and get as close to the edge of the forest as you can without being seen. When you're set, Stig can fly back and give me the word and I'll set this tree on fire," Kate said. "That might draw the Bolliwogs to it, like they were drawn to our campfire. Once they move toward the tree, you can make a break out of the forest. Then, I can follow along after you."

"No, Kate, you can't do that," Eric said. "It's too much of a risk. I mean, how're you gonna make it back with the Bolliwogs chasing you?"

"I should be the one to do it," Stig said. "I can outfly them pretty easily."

"But they won't follow you," Kate said. "It has to be someone on the ground. Besides, you wouldn't be able to light the fire."

"It's still too dangerous, Kate," Eric said, then took a deep breath. "I'll do it."

"No, Eric," Kate's voice was firm and her eyes blazed. "I *have* to do it. It looks like those creatures probably killed my ancestor, and I want to get them!"

"I think I know of a way t' keep 'em from chasin' ya," Hallo said, laughing. "We got some black powder the king give us, right?"

"Yeah," Eric said, and then he laughed, too. "You think we should use it?"

"No time like the present, m' lad," Hallo cackled. "We can tie it t' the outside o' this here tree. We build the fire here, in the center o' the tree, an' when it burns through, it'll give them brutes a scare, don't ya know. It may or mayn't kill 'em, but I don't think they'll be in any shape t' follow us."

They stacked wood inside the tree, and Eric showed Kate how to strike a spark with flint. When everything was ready, Eric took Kate's pack as well as his own, leaving her with just a glowmoss torch.

Then the boy, the dwarf and the owl left the tree and crept through the forest, keeping their torches under wraps. Stig flew ahead to scout. They caught up with him about fifteen minutes later.

"This is about as far as it's safe to go," the owl said. "I'll fly back to Kate and tell her to light the fire. Once it's lit, we'll move a little way off and hide as well as we can."

"What should we do here?" Eric asked.

"Get behind a tree and stay as still as possible. You should be able to see at least a glow from the burning tree. After the bats pass overhead, wait a minute and then run for it, that way," Stig pointed a wing straight ahead. "Kate and I will catch up when we can. When you get to the edge of the forest, you'll see the base of the mountain. I think you should make for that. I'm certain the Jewel is at or near the top."

Eric's heart sank. The thought of having to climb a mountain made him shiver. He took a deep breath. "Okay," was all he said.

Stig nodded. "Right. I'll be off, then. Good luck."

"Good luck," Hallo said as the owl flew away. All Eric could do was nod to his friend.

Hallo looked Eric up and down. "Now listen, lad, don't worry none 'bout that mountain," Hallo smiled. "We'll all he'p ya get up."

Eric nodded again and gave the dwarf a faint smile.

The two crouched still as statues in the silent forest for some time. Eric hardly dared to breathe as they waited for the signal. After ten or fifteen minutes, he felt his legs cramping up and shifted his position to get some relief.

A flickering light grew in the distance behind them. Eric looked over at Hallo. In the dancing yellow light, the dwarf flashed him a smile.

"Look sharp, lad," Hallo whispered. "Lay yerself flat ag'in this tree 'til them creatures goes by."

Eric nodded and pressed his body against the tree.

Soon he heard a noise like thunder, and the Bolliwogs, hundreds of them, passed overhead in the direction of the crackling fire.

Eric and Hallo crouched behind the trees for a few minutes after they had passed. Then Hallo looked at Eric.

"Time t' get goin', don't ya know," the dwarf said, and ran off toward the forest's edge.

Eric jumped up and ran after him. The light from the fire was just bright enough to see by. They ran together, dodging the dead trees. From behind, Eric heard a loud boom, like a clap of thunder. The ground shook a little from the force of the blast, and Eric knew that the fire had reached the black powder strung around the tree.

The boy and the dwarf kept running. Eric wondered if the Bolliwogs had been blown up, or at least stunned. He tried not to wonder if his friends had been caught in the blast, and hoped both Kate and Stig were heading to meet them at the forest's edge.

He expected to hear the thunder of wings at any moment, but after what seemed only a few minutes, both he and Hallo broke free of the forest. They both skidded to a stop and looked around.

The yellow glow from the fire behind them had been replaced by the all-too-familiar red glow. Behind them, the forest fanned out on either side, a dark impenetrable mass. Dead trees stood like petrified soldiers. Although everything was silent, Eric could smell the faint odor of wood smoke from the fire in the woods.

Ahead of them, set off a little way from the forest and a little to their left, a huge mountain rose from the otherwise flat landscape. Eric craned his neck in an effort to see the top, but it was too high. From high above, the red light shone down on the whole land.

The boy was filled with a sense of dread at the sight of that brooding mass of rock. It was taller by far than a skyscraper, and there was something familiar about it that made him feel uneasy.

Eric was snapped out of his reverie by a tug on his pants. "C'mon lad," Hallo said. "We can't stand here gawkin'. Let's make for that mountain like the bird said."

He nodded, and together they ran toward it. As they came closer, he saw the beginning of a path at the base. He headed toward it, Hallo following behind.

After the shelter of the forest, Eric felt exposed in the open. He kept glancing back over his shoulder to reassure himself they weren't being chased.

When they reached the path, they hid themselves among some boulders that were heaped to either side of it, and settled down to wait.

Soon Hallo, who was keeping watch, tapped Eric. "Look sharp, m' lad. Looks like they made it."

Eric looked where the dwarf pointed, and saw Kate running across the open plain, with Stig flying above her. Eric pulled out his torch, waved it over his head a few times, then put it away.

Stig spotted it and guided Kate to where the others were hiding. Her face was flushed with excitement.

"Wow!" was all she could say as she gasped for breath.

"Well, it's real good t' see you 'uns, lass." Hallo was grinning. "We didn't know if we'd ever set eyes on both o' ya ag'in."

"Yeah," Eric said, "we're glad you made it. What happened?"

"After I left you, I flew back to the tree," Stig said. "That's when Kate lit the fire."

"Boy, it flared up great!" Kate cut in. "The tree was so dry, it burned pretty quickly."

"For a moment we worried that the powder would blow up before our winged friends got there," Stig chuckled, "But it worked out very well. The light attracted them right away, and when they got there—"

"When they got there, boom!" Kate interrupted, smacking her hands together. "Bolliwogs on the ground everywhere!"

"So they got blown up?" Eric asked.

"No, not blown up," Stig said. "Many were stunned from the concussion. It even knocked us off our feet, and we were a good hundred yards away in the woods."

"We felt it, too," Eric said, and Hallo nodded. "So some were knocked out. What about the rest?"

"That's the beautiful part," Kate laughed. "They ran away, or I guess flew away. They flew off back toward the clearing so fast you wouldn't believe it."

Hallo let out a whoop. "Then we ain't got nothin' t' worry 'bout no more," he said.

Eric frowned and looked up at the mountain that towered over them. "There's still the mountain," he murmured.

"Ah, don't worry none 'bout that, lad." Hallo snapped his fingers. "I told ya we'd help ya up, don't ya know. Just like in the Kingdom. Ya can walk on the inside, and we'll walk on the outside."

"Yeah," Kate said, "Don't worry, Eric. It's no problem."

"I don't think it's gonna be that easy," Eric said.

The boy looked at Stig. The owl's golden eyes looked back at him.

"We can't help you this time, Eric," Stig said, his voice soft but firm.

"What do ya mean, ya daft bird?" Hallo exploded. "We can't leave him here."

"Hallo, I think he means that I have to go on by myself," Eric said. "Is that it, Stig?"

"This is something you have to do alone Eric," the owl said. "It's why you were given this Assignment. You've got to conquer your fear."

Eric took a deep breath and nodded. The weight of the whole mountain seemed to be pressing down on him.

"Well, no sense hanging around. I guess I better get started," Eric said, but he made no move toward the path.

"Take care o' yourself, lad." Hallo grabbed Eric's hand and pumped it up and down. "Bring the Jewel back with ya."

"Don't worry, you'll do fine," Kate hugged Eric. "Just be strong."

"Remember what the Gatekeeper told you. You've got it in you; all you have to do is find the courage." Stig looked Eric in the eye. "I believe in you."

Eric nodded, wishing he were as confident. He turned and walked over to the beginning of the path. There he stopped and looked back. He wanted to say something to thank his friends and, at the same time, show he wasn't afraid. But all he could do was wave and say, "Bye." Then he headed up the path.

CHAPTER 25

THE GUARDIAN

The path was wide enough for only two people. Eric hugged the mountainside on the far left of the trail as he walked, keeping as far away as possible from the other side of the path. There was nothing on that side, nothing but a fall to the ground below.

"It's like my dream," Eric thought, trembling.

He crept forward, following the trail as it wound upward. He tried to keep his eyes on the path ahead and away from the cliff's edge, silently cursing his shaking legs. Why should he be so scared?

Eric forgot all that for the moment when he noticed a mist beginning to form. At first, he thought his eyes were playing tricks on him, and he rubbed them. But the higher he went, the thicker the mist got, until it had become a fog. Soon, it was so thick, the reddish light coming from above was nothing more than a rosy glow, and he could hardly make out the path before him.

Now, his body tensed as he walked, and his ears strained as he listened for the sound in his dream, the sound he knew must come— the flap of leathery wings. After walking for a while in this way, he couldn't take the strain and stopped to listen.

But he heard nothing. Just the sound of the wind blowing more fog his way. So he continued his journey. He had no idea how high he was now. The mountain had looked huge from the ground. The light that came from what he guessed was its peak had seemed to be as high as the sun.

But that didn't really matter now. All he could do was to keep following the path while staying as far away as possible from the edge and the nothingness beyond.

As he walked, he thought about many things—the village, his friends waiting for him below, the Gatekeeper, his mother. Mostly, though, his thoughts were of his father. His father would want him to be brave, to face what he had to do.

"Am I strong enough?" he thought. "I don't even know what I have to do, or even if I'm the one who's supposed to do it."

He sighed and thought of going back. Then he heard it. The sound he most dreaded. The flap of leathery wings. But not any wings. Huge wings. Just as in his dream.

And yet, not as in his dream. After waking from that dream each time, he'd thought they were the wings of a dragon. But now, he knew better. They were bat's wings. They sounded just like the wings of the Bolliwogs that had chased them, only bigger, much bigger.

And so, this time he was ready when the monster came. The beast tore through the fog, coming at him from behind. Eric looked back. Its red eyes glowed, and venom dripped from yellow fangs. It was big as a dragon, and black hair covered its body. Its pointed ears were laid flat against its head as it swooped down to grab Eric with its clawed feet.

But Eric was ready. He stopped looking back and ran. Ahead of him, the path had straightened and the fog was thinning. The red light was very bright now, so bright he was almost blinded. He thought he could make out the mouth of a cave looming up before him. He felt the hot breath of the giant Bolliwog on his back and could no longer feel his legs. He just kept pumping them as he ran.

He was almost at the cave now. Only it wasn't a cave. Eric caught a glimpse of high stone walls as he passed under an arch; then he was running over cobblestones instead of the dusty path he'd been following. After running through the arch, he stopped, and looked back. His pursuer gave a loud shriek and veered away from the fortress, unable, Eric realized with relief, to follow.

He found himself in a courtyard. The archway he'd run through was set in a huge wall that encircled the mountaintop. The dull, gray stone of the wall loomed up forty feet. In the center of the courtyard, a tower reared up like a bony finger pointing to the sky.

The tower was made of the same gray stone as the outer wall. The red light, bright and clear now, Eric noted, shone from the top of the tower. At its base was set a large wooden door. Seated to the right of the door was a lone figure.

From where he stood, about a third of the way between the wall and the tower, Eric could not tell if it was a living person or a statue made of the same dull gray stone as everything else in the fortress.

Eric took a few tentative steps toward the tower, when the figure spoke. "Come, boy," it croaked, "you've made it this far, let's not dawdle."

Eric crossed the courtyard to the tower door. The figure appeared to be a man. He was ancient, bent by the years, but he was still enormous. Although he was sitting, Eric thought he must be close to ten feet tall. He was dressed in a shapeless tunic of gray. Hoary hands clasped the top of a wooden cane that propped him up. His gray hair was long and greasy; his face, a mass of wrinkles. A bulbous nose jutted over drooping jowls. His eyes were gray, and his bloodless lips formed a slight smile as he gazed at the boy.

"Who are you?" Eric asked.

"I am the Guardian," the giant said. "Actually, I am one of the Guardians. There were twelve. I am the last."

"What do you guard?"

"The Jewel," the Guardian said.

"How long have you guarded it?"

"Since the world was formed," the Guardian replied.

Eric was about to ask another question when the Guardian held up his hand.

"Enough, boy," he said. "It is I who must ask the questions. Are you ready?"

"I think so," Eric said.

"Good." The Guardian nodded. "Let us begin."

The Guardian shifted on his chair, sat a little taller.

"Who sent you?" he asked.

Eric frowned as a bunch of answers flashed through his mind; the dwarf king, the Lord Mayor, Stig. None of those seemed right, though. His answer was more like a question, "The Gatekeeper?"

The Guardian's wrinkled face wrinkled even more in a smile. "Correct," he said. "What do you seek?"

This one seemed easy enough. "The Jewel," Eric said.

"Correct," the Guardian replied. "For what purpose?"

As with the first question, Eric was unsure of the answer. To stop the fighting? No, it must be more than that. To fulfill the Assignment? No, too vague.

The Guardian sat silent. His clear gray eyes were intent as he watched the boy.

Eric could feel himself sweating as he thought. He thought of the tyranny of the pirates, the coldness of dwarven law, and the desolation of the dead forest. He wiped the sweat from his eyes and said, "To heal this world."

The Guardian's smile grew wider. "Correct. Now then, one more. How will *you* be healed?"

Eric's mind reeled. What did the Guardian mean? What healing did he need? Even as he asked himself these questions, in his heart he knew what the Guardian was asking. But Eric didn't think he had an answer for the question. Then he remembered his conversation with the Gatekeeper—it seemed years ago now.

"Listen to me, boy," the Gatekeeper had said. "What happened to your father wasn't your fault. There wasn't anything you could have done to keep him from falling, so stop beating yourself up about it."

"I, I guess," he hesitated. "I guess I've got to forgive myself."

The Guardian's smile grew wider still. He gestured toward the door, and it opened. "Enter. May you find what you seek."

Eric's heart leapt with unexplainable joy as he walked past the Guardian and into the tower. A flight of stone stairs circled up into the darkness above. Eric took his glowmoss torch out of his bag and began the ascent.

As he climbed, he thought about the Guardian's final question. Everyone from his mother to the Gatekeeper had forgiven him for his father's death. In fact, no one had blamed him in the first place. So why was it so hard to accept? Maybe because he, out of everyone, had been right there when it had happened. He was the only one who could have done something.

But was there really anything that he could have done? If he had stuck out his hand, would his father have been able to grab it? And if his father had, would Eric have been strong enough to pull him to safety? Or would he have been pulled over the edge, too?

He must be almost to the top now, he thought. The light from his torch was dim, but there was a reddish glow coming from above that was getting stronger the higher he climbed. His legs ached, but he took no notice. He was still thinking.

The truth was, there wasn't much he could have done that day on the cliff. In fact, he had done everything he could. It was he who had run back to camp for help, faster than he had ever run in his life—including when the Bolliwogs were chasing him.

Because of that, the helicopter had arrived while there was still a chance. His father hadn't made it, but at least Eric had given him that one chance. Now Eric realized it was the best that he could have done.

Eric smiled, and found he had come to the end of the stair. Before him, there was another door. He gave it a push, and it swung in without a sound to reveal a chamber. In its center, the boy saw a pedestal of gray marble. Sunk halfway into the top of the pedestal was a blood-red gem. The red light it gave off almost blinded him. The Jewel was multifaceted and as big around as a pizza.

When Eric stepped into the chamber, it seemed to him as if the very air throbbed with power. He felt drawn to the Jewel and, before he realized it, he stood before it looking into its depths. As he gazed at it, he realized he was looking into the center of the world.

He saw pain there, and anguish. At the root, though, Eric saw—or felt—betrayal. He was now sure the Jewel was calling him with a longing so strong he could not resist. It seemed the most natural thing in the world to wrap his arms around it.

When he did, he felt a jolt. A tingling feeling started in his hands, traveled up his arms and spread to his entire body, making his hair feel as if it was standing on end. The Jewel's red glow surrounded him.

Eric felt the menace in that glow. It threatened to consume him. Then, like a storm that has spent all its energy, the menace of the Jewel subsided. Eric felt numb as the color of the Jewel and the glow that surrounded him began to change. The red became purple, then blue and then green.

When the Jewel glowed green, Eric released his grip on it. A feeling of elation coursed through his whole being. "Yes!" he said in a half whisper. It was all he could think of to say.

"Well done, child," a voice said.

Eric turned, and saw the Guardian filling the doorway. Now that he was standing, Eric saw that the ancient creature was indeed ten feet tall. But the boy thought the Guardian did not look quite so old as before. His smile was broad and he seemed to be less burdened.

"What happened?" Eric asked.

"The Jewel has been restored and made clean," the Guardian said. "It took you, an Outsider, to undo the hurt that was done eons ago."

"What is the Jewel?" Eric looked at the green gem, which now radiated contentment.

"It was placed here when the world was made," the ancient creature said. "Guiding events when needed to make sure the world continues to grow and evolve."

"You mean like a compass?"

The Guardian shook its head. "Just the opposite. The Jewel is the pole by which history steers. When the Jewel was tampered with, events had no direction and there was no more growth."

"How did that happen?"

"The Guardians were given the task of protecting the Jewel by the Creator. There were twelve of us originally—Merrill, Quillius, Harrell, Ovid, Arsenenon, Jorvill, Kensit, Xenpheril, Garvot, Dimset, Clovis and myself, Sophus. We were charged to guard the Jewel according to the High Law.

"It was we who built the tower and the keep. We also built twelve houses of stone, set in a circle near the edge of the forest. In those days, the forest was lush and green, the sky blue and clear, and the land bountiful."

"Paradise," Eric murmured.

"Yes, I suppose it was," the Guardian said. "Or something very close to it. We shared the forest with many different creatures, including a race of tree dwellers that we called simply, the Tree Folk. Wise in woodcraft were they and gentle of spirit. They were good company to us in our vigil, and good friends. Together, we shared everything, according to the Law, each taking no more than was necessary and each giving what was needed.

"Life continued thus for many an age, and we were all content. But all that changed. You see, our eyes were turned outward, we never expected treachery from within.

"One of us, our brother Clovis, sought to set himself above the Law.

Late one night when he had the watch, Clovis crept into the chamber and tried to take the Jewel for himself. Looking back, the Jewel must have been weighing on his mind for centuries. You see, he craved the power he thought the Jewel could give him." The Guardian sighed.

"Poor fool. He planned to unleash that power and enslave the world. But, unknown to any of us, one final safeguard had been laid upon the Jewel by the Creator, should the Guardians ever fail.

"The moment Clovis touched the Jewel, there was a large explosion and the Jewel turned a deep red. Clovis disappeared, and all the land from here to what men call the Iron Mountains was laid waste. The Tree Folk were transformed to Bolliwogs, doomed to haunt their beloved forest. Some civilizations were cut off from one another, while others splintered and sought dominance. And we," the Guardian sighed again, "We grew old and gray, trying to atone for the crime of our brother. One by one my brothers have fallen, until now I, Sophus, am the last."

"What about the giant Bolliwog that chased me here?" Eric asked.

"He is Elborat, the king of the Tree Folk," the Guardian said. "He and his people have waited a long time to be liberated."

"What happened to the other Guardians?"

"They faded, worn down by the weight and pain of our brother's betrayal. Only I, Sophus, whose name in the Ancient Tongue means 'steadfast,' have endured." The Guardian said this last without any hint of pride or boasting. But it seemed to Eric that a trace of weariness had returned to the ancient creature for a moment.

"Some came with the hope of winning the Jewel," the Guardian continued. "Most of these were dwarves. But they were under the impression that the Jewel was a thing to be won—a trophy or talisman. It is not. One alone there was who came here with honest intent."

"Cal Endria. So he made it through the forest," Eric whispered.

The Guardian nodded. "He made it, although the Bolliwogs tried to keep him away."

"What happened to him?" Eric asked.

"He came and I asked him his questions," the Guardian said.

"His questions?" the boy asked.

"Each who comes does so for their own purpose. So, therefore, the questions change for each," the Guardian said. "I liked him. He was a good man, and he was true to his purpose. But he was not the one, not a true Outsider. His purpose was too narrow, and so he ceased to be.

"And now," the Guardian said, brightening a bit, "let's be done with questions for the moment. I believe your friends have come to seek you."

There was a noise on the stairs, and Kate and Hallo came into the chamber, followed by Stig, who perched on a window ledge.

"It seems our quest has met with some success," Stig said as he looked at the Jewel. "We were hiding in the rocks at the bottom of the mountain and that blood-red light was shining down. There was a tingling in the air, it almost vibrated, and then the whole world was transformed. We were standing in a field of the greenest grass I've ever seen and the sky was blue."

"Yeah, an' the forest weren't dead no more. The trees was all alive an' growin'. Looked like a right homey place, too. Then, these folk comes right out o' the forest. They was tall, taller than the Big Folk, but shorter 'un this fella here," Hallo said, jerking a thumb at the Guardian. "You're a tall 'un, ain't ya? Anyways, they looked a little green 'round the gills, don't ya know, and they had these pointy faces and ears, but they was friendly.

"They said, 'Your friend has been successful, your quest is completed and we have been liberated. Go up and greet him.' Then they turned 'round and went back inta the forest, just like that. It was the darndest—"

It was then he caught sight of the Jewel. "Well, I'll be et for a tater!" Hallo gazed in wide-eyed wonder at the brilliant green gem. "It's the Jewel, don't ya know. M' pappy'll never believe it."

All the while, Kate had been staring at the stone in silence. Now she gave Eric a questioning look. Eric shook his head, and Kate burst into tears. Eric went over to her and held her as she sobbed.

"Now, now, child," the Guardian said. "As I've just finished telling the boy, your ancestor was a good and brave man. He just was not the one. What were you expecting?"

Kate turned her tear-streaked face up to the Guardian. "I, I was half hoping he'd be here waiting for us. I've heard so much about him during my life, about how he left and never returned, that I thought maybe he hadn't ever died. That he would lead us through the mountains like he wanted."

"In a way he did, Kate," Eric said. "In a way he did. He blazed the trail."

" 'Scuse me. m' lord," Hallo said to the Guardian. "Can I just touch the Jewel? I'd like t' be the one that carries it t' the Kingdom, but if'n that's the duty o' the lad, it'd still be a' honor among m' people if'n I could just lay one o' m' fingers on it."

"The only one who may touch the Jewel is the Outsider," the Guardian said. "But even he may not move it. Its place is here, and here it shall stay until the ending of the world."

"But if we can't take the Jewel," Kate left Eric to stand before the Guardian, "how will we get the help of the dwarves and save my village?"

"Perhaps just returning from beyond the Forbidden Door will be enough to get them to help us, Kate," Eric said.

"Nay, lad," Hallo shook his head, "the king'll want nothin' but the Jewel. It's what he sent us for, an' what we got t' bring back, don't ya know."

The Guardian's face erupted wrinkles as he frowned. "How would it be, master dwarf, if you were to bring a piece of the Jewel back with you?"

"Aye, that might be good enough," the dwarf said. "But how d' ya propose t' chip a piece off if'n no one can touch it?"

"While the world was being made, the Creator cut the jewel from the stuff of which the world is formed. He polished the Jewel and cut it like a jeweler cuts a diamond—twelve facets it has, one for each of the Guardians. The Maker took the pieces that he cut from the Jewel and set them in twelve rings. Then he gave each of the Guardians one of the rings."

The Guardian held up his left hand, and they saw he wore a golden ring with a large green stone set in the top.

"Outsider, you may not take the Jewel, but I will offer you my ring," the Guardian said, and he slipped the ring off his finger and held it out to Eric.

Eric took the ring. A jagged piece of the Jewel was set into it, held by five prongs of gold. The stone was the same green as the Jewel and, while it glowed, it did so with less intensity than the larger gem. When Eric held the ring, it gave off the same calm feeling that radiated from the Jewel.

Eric wasn't sure what to do with it, although he knew enough not to slip it into his pocket.

"Here lad," a voice at his elbow said. Hallo held a fine gold chain out to him. "Hang that piece o' jewelry 'round your neck with this."

"Thanks, Hallo," Eric said as he took the chain and threaded it through the ring. Then he clasped the chain around his neck and tucked it under his shirt.

"Sophus," Eric asked, "what happened to Clovis's ring when he touched the Jewel? Was it destroyed?"

"No, it disappeared with Clovis, but it could not have been destroyed. The rings are part of the Jewel and cannot be destroyed while the world lasts."

"Well, I think it's time we got going," Stig said. "The world may be back on course, but I daresay the pirates are still running amok through Calendria."

"Yeah," Eric frowned, "I was hoping everything would be put right when the Jewel turned color, but I guess that'd be too easy, wouldn't it?"

"I think so," Stig nodded. "This is something we all have to do together, I think."

"Yeah," Kate wiped the tears from her face. "We've got to get moving. It's been a while, and I don't think the village will be able to hold out too long."

"What're we lollygaggin' 'round here for, then?" Hallo asked. "Let's get goin'."

The Guardian led them all down the tower stairs. When they reached the courtyard, Eric saw that it had changed. The sun shone bright from a blue sky. The gray stone walls were hung with beautiful banners in breathtaking colors. The stones themselves were no longer dull, but shone like silver.

The Guardian saw them through the outer gate. "Farewell, children," he said, "may your quest be successful."

"Thank you, Sophus," Eric said, "I think your gift will help it to be successful."

Sophus raised a bony hand in farewell. Eric, Stig, Kate and Hallo waved, turned, and went down the mountain. Eric noticed that he no longer felt any fear at being up so high, just a sense of calm resolve. He smiled until he looked out over the forest to the Iron Mountains beyond. He set his jaw. Their task was not yet done.

CHAPTER 26

ENDINGS

The siege of the village had left the defenders exhausted, but determined. Although the pirates had laid waste to the harbor and the houses and farms along the main road leading up to the Green, the villagers had hung tough, rolling lighted barrels of black powder down the hill, causing confusion in the pirates' camp.

As the days went by, Sharky had become more and more enraged. Finally, in a fit of frustrated anger, he ordered his men to charge the barricade at the top of the hill. Wave after wave of pirates stormed the hill, only to be repulsed by a storm of arrows.

Finally, Mr. Marrow took his captain aside. "I think it's time to change our strategy, Captain," Mr. Marrow said.

"What d'ya mean," Sharky barked. "I'll beat that rabble inta submission if it takes every last one o' me crew!"

"I know, Captain. You're very determined," Mr. Marrow cooed. "But there may be another way."

"How?"

"We've been concentrating all our forces on a frontal assault," the first mate said. "That's what they expect. But perhaps we should come at them from the flank."

"Explain," Sharky growled, getting interested.

"I'll take half the men down to the mouth of the river and come up through the farms. We'll take the bridge and storm onto the Green by climbing up the far side of the hill. While we're taking them by surprise, you can send the rest of the lads up the hill. We'll be pushing from the front and the side..."

"And we'll crush 'em," Sharky crowed. "Mr. Marrow, yer a genius. Round up them dogs an' get 'em movin'!"

⁊⊘⊂⅋

The next day, the Lord Mayor was meeting with the Council in the meeting hall. He shook his head as he looked around the table. There was not one Council member who had escaped unscathed in some way or another.

While it was obvious the battle had been hard on them, still, the Lord Mayor thought, they did not look beaten. In fact, they all wore the same look of grim determination. It was a look that reflected the attitude of the entire village. While it remained to be seen who the final victors would be, the Lord Mayor was certain his village would not give up. That thought filled him with pride.

"We're tired, ladies and gentlemen," he said. "But we are not defeated. You've done a great job, and I feel sure that help is not too far off. But, we must plan for the worst. We've got to keep up the fight, for we have nowhere else to go.

"Okay, let's get to the status reports. Cordon, Atticus, how are the defenses holding up, and what's the weapons situation?"

The blacksmith and the stonemason rose. Cordon's head sported a bandage that made him look as if he were wearing a turban. Mr. Flint's arms and hands were scraped and bruised, both from the fighting and from his work on the stone walls.

182

"Well now, Charles, the wall's holding up pretty well, if I do say so myself." Mr. Flint gave a slight smile. "Those spikes Cordon rigged up mean they can't get near it so long as it's defended. We're a little weak on our left flank, but it'd be hard going uphill through a lot of underbrush to hit us that way, I'm thinking."

"Our powder's just about gone, Charles," the large blacksmith said. "The arrow supply isn't much better."

"How much longer will both last, do you think?" the Lord Mayor asked.

"A few days at best," Cordon said.

"I think I can help in the arrow department," Nan said. "But it's a little risky."

"Well, we're at the point where everything is risky, Nan," the Lord Mayor told the net mender. "What's your plan?"

"When it gets dark, I'll take a few of the archers and slip over the wall," she said. "We'll sneak down the hill a little way and collect some of our arrows. If we do this each night, we'll be all right as far as arrows are concerned."

"Okay, Nan, but be careful. I don't want to lose anyone by taking too great a risk. Now, Mrs. Casker, what's the situation with the villagers?"

"They're holding up as well as can be expected," she said. "Charles, our people will fight as long as they have to. Deep down, these are tough folk. We're not going to be pushed out of here by a bunch of rabble."

The Lord Mayor was about to reply when a villager burst into the Council Chamber. "Lord Mayor, the pirates are attacking!" he shouted.

"That's nothing new, Lamkin," Cordon growled, "We're in the middle of a Council."

"But they've flanked us, Cordon," Lamkin said. "They're attacking both our front and our left. They've gotten in from the side and are set to overwhelm us!"

At that, the Lord Mayor and the entire Council rushed out of the building. The sight that met them was one of confusion. It looked as if the pirates were routing the villagers. One group with Mr. Marrow at their head was storming up the hill from the river valley, while another group led by Sharky was climbing over the wall.

The villagers had turned to meet the pirates streaming in to the left, only to be set upon by the group coming from the center. As a result, Sharky's men had almost surrounded the defenders at the wall. The remaining villagers were coming from their posts to help, but things looked bad to the Lord Mayor.

Cordon, Atticus Flint and Nan ran toward the wall to try to restore some sort of order. Twigg, Furrow and Mrs. Casker went to the Lord Mayor's house to help with the wounded.

Madame Bottleneck was going to follow them, but the Lord Mayor grabbed her arm.

"Charles, what are you doing?" Madame Bottleneck said. "The wounded are my responsibility. I have to see to them."

"Just one minute, Moira." There was weariness in the Lord Mayor's eyes. "Everything's falling apart, isn't it?"

"Did you really believe it wouldn't?" Her voice was harsh, but the look in her eyes was tender. "Charles, these aren't warriors. They're simple people pitted against a ruthless foe. They've fought hard for what's theirs, but eventually it had to end this way. What did you expect?"

"Oh, I don't know," he sighed. "I hoped that Kate and the rest would get help from the Dwarf Kingdom. But we've heard nothing. I don't even know if they're still alive."

184

The apothecary gave her friend a sympathetic look. "We've got our jobs to do, Charles. I know you're worried about her—about all of them—but you can't worry about what's not in your control."

The Lord Mayor sighed again and nodded. They were about to part when they heard a low rumble coming from the direction of the mountains. Everyone, friend and foe alike, heard it as well. Something was moving toward the village from beyond the far end of the Green. The fighting stopped as everyone turned their eyes to stare at a large cloud of dust that rose above the Lord Mayor's house, blotting out the mountains beyond.

The rumble became the tramp of hundreds of marching feet over which the sound of singing could be heard, although no one could make out the words. Then, an army of dwarves emerged from behind the Lord Mayor's house. They were armed for battle with axe, sword and shield. Some were clad in red mail, while others wore mail of blue or gray. With them were tall, greenish creatures that looked like men, but taller and leaner.

At the head of the army came King Angus Thunderhelm, in golden armor. At his side marched one of the tall creatures, clad in green armor and a silver crown. Beside them was Hallo and another, older dwarf. Kate and Eric were there, too, and Stig flew above them. Hallo, Kate and Eric carried axes and small, round shields. The Lord Mayor thought he saw a brilliant green light springing from Eric's chest.

As the dwarves marched, they sang:

"We come, we come,
With clash of axe and beat of drum,
To banish sorrow and end despair,
To chase the pirates back to their lair.

We come, we come,
Beware the might of the Kingdom!"

A wild surge of joy filled the Lord Mayor. "They've come, they've come!" he shouted, "Behold the Deliverers and my daughter! They bring the King of the Dwarf Kingdom and the Jewel of Paradise!"

"The Deliverers! The dwarves! The Jewel!" the villagers nearest the Lord Mayor shouted. In a moment the chant was on the lips of all the villagers as they felt their strength and hopes revive.

The dwarves swept down onto the Green and headlong into the bewildered pirates. They would surely have broken and fled but for the ferocious Sharky. The pirate captain, mad with battle rage, raced to and fro among his men, kicking, hitting, biting, punching and spitting.

"These ain't nothin' but half men, ye dogs!" he roared. "Have at 'em! Any man what runs'll have to answer to me. I'll hang their hide from the tallest mast!"

The dwarves and their strange allies proved too much for the pirates, however. From the back of the dwarf ranks, a sound like cannon boomed and a hail of shot rained down on the pirates, blowing holes in their lines. The Lord Mayor saw that a group of dwarves held portable cannon in their large, muscled arms. The rest of the dwarves hacked at the pirates with their axes, while the strange green men let loose a stream of arrows.

As the battle raged, the pirates were pushed off the Green and back against the stone wall. Hallo and his father, Jeremiah, fought side by side and the pirates fell back before them. Stig swooped down again and again, pecking at their eyes. Kate was so eager to fight that Eric spent most of his time holding her back, but she managed to get in a few good swings with her axe.

One by one, the pirates began surrendering until one group of twenty-five or so led by Mr. Marrow and Captain Sharky were the only ones still fighting. At their backs, the wall kept them from retreating further. Sharky continued to bully the few men he had left, raining threats and curses down on them to keep them fighting.

But the Captain's forces were dwindling, and soon he was forced to fight on the front line. It was then that a stone, launched from a villager's sling, struck the Captain on the head, dazing him.

Suddenly, Mr. Marrow rushed up from behind, slipped a long length of rope around the Captain's neck, and pulled it tight. Although thin as a skeleton, Mr. Marrow was strong.

"Well, well, Captain, sir," Mr. Marrow cooed into his ear. "This is a bad mess you've gotten us into, isn't it? Doesn't look like there's any way out but one."

"Wha—, what're ye talkin' about, ye daft fool?" Sharky struggled, but Mr. Marrow held him firm.

"I was thinking that perhaps a deal might be arranged with the noble villagers—your head for the freedom of myself and what's left of the boys. These soft villagers will let us go thinking we're beaten, but we'll back and I'll not make a mess of things like you."

"Ye're out o' yer head. So that's it, is it? Ye always wanted t' get rid o' me an' take me place, didn't yer? I'll, ah—" Sharky was cut off as Mr. Marrow pulled the noose tighter.

"There, there Captain, don't speak," Mr. Marrow's voice was slick as oil. "It's only natural once we're out of this that I take command. It's nothing for you to worry about. Soon, you'll be asleep forever, may you rot!"

Marrow twisted the noose one more time. Sharky quivered and went limp, his tongue protruding from foam-flecked lips. Mr. Marrow threw Sharky to the ground, and turned to face the battle.

"Boys, the Captain's dead!" Mr. Marrow said. "That's it, we've had it. Let's throw ourselves on their mercy."

The remaining pirates cheered.

Behind the first mate, Sharky opened his eyes and sat up. He pulled himself to his feet, and pulled a long, curved knife from his belt, the ring on his finger glowing red with his rage. On unsteady legs, the pirate captain crept up on Mr. Marrow from behind.

The cheering pirates had turned to face the first mate. When they saw their captain rise, they fell silent and the blood drained from their faces. Before Mr. Marrow had time to realize what was going on, Sharky grabbed him from behind.

"Marrow, ye should know yer can't kill yer captain that easy. Ye be fergettin' I be Death hisself," Sharky whispered into the first mate's ear as he ran him through. Mr. Marrow's wire-thin body slumped to the ground.

"Now fight, ye dogs!" Sharky roared, insanity flaring in his eyes. "Fight or ye'll 'ave t' deal with me!"

The terrified crew did not know which way to turn. On one side, they faced the advancing villagers, dwarves and tree folk. On the other, there was the terrible wrath of Sharky.

They decided in an instant. The pirates threw down their weapons and ran into the arms of the villagers, who tied them up and led them away.

Now Sharky stood alone. Still raging, he leaped to the top of the wall. "Ye can't take me, an' ye won't!" he raved. "Sharky can't be stopped by a group o' rabble like ye!"

The Lord Mayor stepped forward. "Sharky, give yourself up. You have my word that both you and your men will be treated fairly."

Sharky looked down on him and sneered. "Fair? Why should I believe ye? Ye can keep my men," he snarled. "They're nothin' but spineless jellyfish, just like ye!"

Eric felt the ring throb against his chest. He took the chain from around his neck and laid the ring on his open palm. As he looked at it in his hand, the piece of the Jewel blazed a brilliant green. He knew what to do.

"Sharky!" he yelled. "Give it up. There's nowhere to go!"

"Ye'll never take me!" Sharky snarled. "No boy can best ol' Sharky!"

With a calm that surprised him, Eric twirled the chain over his head like a cowboy with a lariat. When he could hear the ring whistling around his head, Eric let the chain fly. It sailed through the air like a green comet and struck Captain Sharky between the eyes.

For a moment, the pirate leader stood frozen to the spot, encased in a green cloud, an odd look—half hatred, half astonishment—on his face. Then, to Eric's surprise, Sharky grew taller and his face changed. For a moment, Eric thought Sophus stood before him, trapped in the green nimbus. But the face, while definitely that of a Guardian, was harsher, haughtier.

But even as Eric was thinking this, the Guardian's face softened into a smile.

"Thank you, Outsider, for releasing me," the figure said.

"You're Clovis." Eric stated. "And you're Sharky, too."

"Yes."

"How?" Eric asked.

"I was arrogant. I sought to seize the power of the Jewel and rule the world. I thought it my right, my destiny. But the Creator was wise. When I laid hands on the Jewel, and my ring made contact with it, I was hurled half a world away, trapped within it.

"The ring was found by a wicked man, and I was able to exercise limited control over him. I stayed with him for decades, but he did

189

not have access to the power I desired, for I still sought power.

"So the ring and I moved on to other wicked men over the centuries, but no one was worthy. Until one day when I found someone truly evil."

"Sharky." Eric whispered.

"Aye, Sharky—someone who desired power and domination almost as much as I. Through Sharky, I was able to terrorize and control half the world with his pirate band."

"But not the entire world," Stig observed.

"No, the mountains still thwarted me. But I put the thought in his head to let Cal Endria and his band settle there, thinking perhaps they would find a route through the mountains. I also put the thought that the mountains were a challenge worthy of him into Sharky's head. After dealing with the village, he would have turned his attention to them, but the Outsider beat him to it."

"So what now?" Eric asked.

"The path of the world has been set right. My ring now glows with the green of paradise as does your ring and the Jewel itself."

"And what of you?" Stig asked. "Will you go to join your brother Guardians?"

Clovis shook his huge ancient head. "I must go to judgment before the Creator. I regret my actions. Only now do I see how arrogant and foolish I've been. I hope the Creator will be merciful."

With that, Clovis raised a hand in farewell and disappeared, leaving only the crumpled husk of Sharky.

"So ends the reign of the evil Sharky," the Lord Mayor said, and the villagers cheered.

Stig perched on the wall next to Eric, and the Lord Mayor proclaimed, "Behold, the Deliverers!" The villagers cheered once more. Eric blushed.

"Papa!" Kate ran to the Lord Mayor, and they hugged. "We did it!"

"Behold my daughter, Kate Endria!" the Lord Mayor said to the crowd. "Who better to lead you after I am gone?"

"No one! No one!" the villagers roared. "She will be the Lady Mayor!"

Kate smiled and hugged her father again. Then, she hugged Eric, Stig, and Hallo.

"Lord Mayor, I'd like to introduce His Majesty, Angus Thunderhelm, king of the Dwarf Kingdom, and His Majesty, Elborat, king of the Tree Folk, whose people live in the Great Forest beyond the mountains," Eric said.

"It's an honor to know your majesties," the Lord Mayor said as he shook the hand of each in turn. "Your coming has delivered our people. I can't express our gratitude enough."

"Aw, that's all right. It's the young 'uns an' the bird that ya should praise," King Angus said.

"That's the truth of it," the king of the Tree Folk said in a rich, melodious voice. Then he gave a wry smile. "They have performed a great service, greater than any of the heroes of old. Besides that, they rescued me from life as a winged rodent."

The dwarves and the Tree Folk helped the villagers begin the task of tearing down the wall, dealing with the prisoners, and rebuilding. Help also came from an unexpected source.

" 'Scuse me, m' lord," one of the prisoners said to Cordon as they were being rounded up to be taken to a cell in the iron mines. "M' name's Fishbane. Me an' some o' the boys was wondrin' if we could be o' service—help w' the diggin' an' buildin' an' all."

Cordon looked at the former pirate and the other prisoners. "Is this true? Do you want to make amends for your cursed evil?"

The majority of the pirates nodded.

"Well then," Cordon said, "you'd be welcome to help, provided you don't try any tricks. I'll have some stout fellows watching to make sure you don't."

"Why'd we want t' do that, yer honor? Sharky were the blackest villain in these here waters. Yer've taken 'im out o' the picture, an' we're grateful t' yer. I ain't a-feared o' no man, 'cept 'im, an' the boys feel the same," Fishbane said.

At the end of the day, the Lord Mayor invited the two kings to dinner at his house. They declined, saying they needed to see to their folk, who were camped on the Green. Jeremiah Tosis, who had not left his son's side during the battle, joined the four travelers and Madame Bottleneck for dinner with the Lord Mayor.

When they arrived at the house, Gretchen gave each of the travelers a hug—even Hallo. Over dinner, they told the story of their journey into the Kingdom, beyond the mountains and in the tower of the Heart of the World.

The Lord Mayor and Madame Bottleneck gazed on Eric with looks of awe as he told of the moment he touched the Jewel of Paradise and, with that touch, restored it.

"I'd give anything to see it," Madame Bottleneck said.

"The way is open now," Kate said. "According to the Guardians, now that the Jewel has been restored, the peoples of the world won't be closed off from each other. The dwarves will let us pass through the Kingdom on the Main Avenue, and the Tree Folk will let travelers through the Great Forest. There will be pilgrimages now to gaze into the Heart of the World, just like there were thousands of years ago."

"Yep, and m' son's the one what's gonna be in charge o' traffic through the Kingdom," Jeremiah Tosis slapped his son on the back.

"You've been reinstated, I take it," the Lord Mayor said to Hallo.

Hallo grinned. "We ain't never needed a' ambassador before. An' who'd a thought what I were doin' while I was exiled was bein' a diplomat, but that's what it were. I guess that's m' talent, don't ya know."

"Kate, a minute ago, you talked of the Guardians, but I thought there was only one left," Madame Bottleneck said.

Kate and the others then told the story of their return journey. After taking their leave of the Guardian, they made their way back down the mountain. They reached the bottom and entered the forest, which was now bursting with life. The leafy treetops rustled in a gentle breeze. Birds chirped and squirrels chased each other up and down trees, and across the forest floor.

There they met King Elborat and some of the Tree Folk. The king told them that he and his people would come to Calendria's aid. So it was that the four friends continued their journey with the army of the Tree Folk behind them.

Next, they came upon the clearing, which had also undergone a dramatic change. Eleven of the twelve dwellings were restored. The beauty of the large stone buildings still had Hallo shaking his head as he told this part of their story.

"Them buildin's were grander than anythin' I ever seen our folk do," the dwarf said. "M' folk still have a thing or two t' learn, although I didn't know it 'til I saw them buildin's."

In the clearing, they were greeted by the other ten Guardians, Merrill, Arsenenon, Jorvill, Kensit, Xenpheril, Garvot, Quillius, Harrell, Ovid and Dimset. All were younger than Sophus, who still carried the cares of his constant vigil.

The group had continued on through the forest until they came to the Iron Mountains. Here, King Elborat told his army to wait outside until he received permission from the dwarf king to pass through the Kingdom.

The four travelers and the king of the Tree Folk had gone up the passage and through the Forbidden Door into the throne room, much to the surprise of King Angus Thunderhelm. After the initial shock had worn off, the dwarf king marshaled his forces and the two armies had issued forth from the Main Gate and on to victory.

When their story was done, the Lord Mayor gazed at them, a bemused smile on his face.

"Well, Eric and Stig, it looks as if my daughter was right; you are the Deliverers," he said.

"We couldn't have done it without Kate and Hallo," Eric said.

"Quite right," Stig agreed. "They did play an important part. You and the villagers can't be overlooked, either. You believed in us and held out against Sharky until we could arrive with help."

"What will you two do now?" Madam Bottleneck asked.

"I'd like to help get things cleaned up here," Eric said.

"Yes, that is the proper thing," Stig said. "We'll help you make a start, then we'll have to be going back."

"Going back!" Kate said. "I thought you'd both stay."

"That's not the way it works," Stig said.

"Yeah, I gotta go back. My mom's going to be worried enough as it is," Eric said with a grin. He was trying to make light of it, but he had a sinking feeling in the pit of his stomach at the thought of leaving his friends.

CHAPTER 27

HOMEWARD BOUND

Eric and Stig spent the next week helping to clear the wreckage of the pirate siege. When the debris had been cleared and tents erected for those whose homes had to be rebuilt, the dwarves and the Tree Folk returned home. Eric knew the time had come for him to return home as well.

He and Stig said their good-byes to the Council and the villagers. Then, escorted by the Lord Mayor, Kate and Hallo, they retraced the path they followed on the day they arrived, seemingly a long time ago to Eric. When they reached the beach where they met Kate, they located the stream and made their way along it through the jungle until they saw the door. The strange sight seemed familiar to him—like home.

"Wow, I don't believe it," Kate said.

"It's one o' the strangest sights I ever laid eyes on, don't ya know," Hallo said.

"Until now, I think there was a part of me that still didn't quite believe that you were from another world," the Lord Mayor said. "But this is the final proof, I'd say."

They all stood there for a moment, no one wanting to be the first to say goodbye.

Finally, the Lord Mayor extended his hand. "I guess this is good-bye, Eric," he said.

"Yeah, I guess it is." Eric reached out and shook.

"Thank you for everything you and Stig have done."

"Thanks for believing in us, sir."

"Goodbye, lad," Hallo said, grabbing Eric in a rough embrace. "You've been a right good friend, an' if ever you're travelin' this way again, be sure t' look me up, don't ya know. An' that goes for you too, birdie!"

"You have my word on that, Hallo," Stig said.

"Yeah, you bet," Eric said. "I'm gonna miss you, Hallo."

Then, Eric turned to Kate and was almost bowled over as she hugged him tight. "Goodbye, Eric. Thanks for everything."

"Uh, g'bye, Kate," Eric stammered. "Thanks for believing in us."

"Yes," Stig agreed, "Without your support, I doubt we would have been able to accomplish anything."

"I just can't believe this is goodbye," Kate said.

"Yeah," Eric said. "It does seem kinda strange."

"Well, you know, it may not be goodbye forever," Stig said.

"You think so?" Eric asked, a strange hope rising.

"In my experience, you can never tell. It could well be that our paths will cross again."

"Well, then I guess I'll just say goodbye for now," said Kate.

"Okay," Eric said. "That sounds better."

"I say, we really must be going," Stig said. "Goodbye, everyone. It really has been most enjoyable getting to know you."

Then, Eric pushed open the door and just like that, he and Stig were back inside the Hallway of Worlds.

It seemed to Eric that it had been years since he was last in the Hallway, so much had happened. He felt very tired.

Suddenly, the familiar desk appeared, still cluttered with paperwork. And there, sitting behind it, was the Gatekeeper. His smile seemed to Eric to be wider than before. The boy answered it with one of his own.

"Well done, Eric, Stig," said the old man as he came around the desk to shake Eric's hand.

"Thanks," Eric said, still smiling. "It was tough, but we did it." He actually couldn't believe it as he thought about it.

"Yes, it was touch and go, but Eric did quite well."

"I couldn't have done it without Stig," Eric said.

"That's the way it's supposed to be, of course," the Gatekeeper replied. "I'm so pleased."

"I still can't believe it."

"I never doubted you could do it," the Gatekeeper replied. "Your father would be proud."

Eric smiled. "Yeah, I guess he would be, wouldn't he?" The thought made him feel light, almost giddy.

"He was always proud of you," the Gatekeeper said.

Eric nodded, a tear sliding down his cheek.

Brushing it away he whispered, "Thanks for giving me the chance."

"You're welcome. Now, I think it's time you were on your way home. Follow me."

The Gatekeeper led Eric and Stig back down the Hallway. Unlike before, the old man seemed to know exactly where he was headed and soon they stood before one of the countless doors.

"Here we are," he said.

The door changed shape, morphing into the round shape of the drainpipe door.

"I guess this is goodbye, Stig," Eric said. He hadn't realized just how much he was going to miss the old bird.

"As I told Hallo and Kate, it is goodbye for now, not forever," Stig said.

"Yeah, but that was just so they wouldn't feel bad, right?" Eric asked.

"Oh, no. The three of you have been on an Assignment now. You never know when you may be called upon again."

"Stig's right," the Gatekeeper said. "You've all been a big help, and if anything else comes up, I'll be calling for you again. That is, if it's all right with you."

"Sure," Eric said. "That'd be great!"

"Well, then. No long goodbyes," Stig said. "Take care and I daresay we'll see each other again soon."

Bolstered by this news, Eric opened the door and went through. It was good to be going home.

ABOUT THE AUTHOR:

Gregory S. Slomba grew up in Connecticut dreaming of being either a children's writer or a major leaguer. When he realized he couldn't hit a fastball, much less a curve, he decided that writing was the thing. After receiving his BA in English from the University of Dayton, he was raring to go. However, fate stepped in, turned everything upside down (as it so often does), and he found himself a banker.

Even so, the dream never really died. While working in the world of finance, he spent 17 years as an advisor to his church's high school youth group, writing them a Christmas story every year. After taking a four year career detour as an editor for a trade magazine, he felt ready to write his first book, which you now hold in your hands. Hopefully, this is just the beginning.

Greg lives in Connecticut with his wife, Stephanie, and his children, Christian and Abigail.

WANT TO LEARN MORE?

Check out Greg's blog at
http://thedelivererssharkeyandthejewel.blogspot.com

Made in the USA
Charleston, SC
28 October 2012